Teased

Jamie Begley

Teased

ISBN-13: 978-0615904184
ISBN-10: 0615904181

Prologue

"Close door one, open door two." Colton could hear the cold voice over the loudspeaker as he watched the doors open in order, knowing it was leading to his freedom.

Taking a deep breath of fresh air, he walked through the metal gate into the parking lot of "The Grange" where several cars were waiting to pick up the newly released prisoners. The maximum-security prison, where he had served his punishment decreed by the court, held hardened criminals. Serving three of his five-year sentence had been hard, but now it was over.

Colton took another deep breath, catching sight of the car waiting for him. King had said he would have someone waiting, however only a sadistic son of a bitch would send the same woman responsible for his incarceration. Tessa stood in her shorts and tank top, leaning against her car. If she didn't get back in the car, one of the other men being released would be going back in before he truly had his freedom back.

"Get in the car, Tessa, you're showing enough ass to get yourself in trouble," Colton ordered.

Tessa made a face before sliding back inside the mustang. Colton opened the car door, ignoring Hank-the-Yank giving him the thumbs up, his greedy eyes still trying to gaze at Tessa through the car windows.

"Why are you here?" Colton asked through gritted teeth while getting into the car.

"Now is that any way to say hello after all this time, Colton? I missed you. When King said you needed a ride, I volunteered." Tessa's overly cheerful voice grated on his nerves.

"I don't need any favors from you." Colton stared out the window, watching the scenery as it passed by. He wanted out of the tight confines of the car with her cloying perfume filling his senses.

Three years without a woman underneath him had been torture. However Tessa sitting next to him had no effect other than making him want to put down the window. King was smart; he had every intention of luring Colton into working for him. Sending Tessa was his reminder that Colton owed him a favor.

This time King's manipulations wouldn't work. Prison had taught him a hard lesson. You had two choices; clean up your shit or keep going down that never-ending road until you were a lifer and died behind those walls.

Colton had learned his lesson. He had no intention of going back.

"You look good. You clean?"

Tessa heard the question in his voice. "I am. Been clean since rehab." Her fingers tightened on the steering wheel. "I told you I would get clean and I have."

Colton nodded his head, not saying anything more. He had given her a chance; it was good to know she had been smart enough to use it.

"I never got the paperwork," Colton said coldly.

"I thought we would wait and see how we felt after you got out. I don't want a divorce," Tessa said softly, looking at him from the corner of her eye.

"I told you to take care of it, you didn't, so now I'll take care of it myself," Colton informed her.

"Colton, give it some time. Let's—" Tessa started to protest.

"Tessa, our marriage was over when I found out you were selling pussy to feed that habit of yours. You almost destroyed my business and you put me in prison. I think our marriage is pretty much in the shitter." Colton's voice left no doubt he hadn't forgiven her during his time in prison.

"The business is good, Colton. Reverend has been doing the ink. I've gotten pretty good at giving tats and piercings. We even pierce cock now." She took her eyes off the road to grin at him, ignoring his harsh words.

"Yeah? That's one job I won't be taking off your hands." Colton's eyes returned to gazing out the window.

Tessa laughed. "Now that we have you back, Green Dragon Tats will rake in even more cash. No one has your skill."

Colton hadn't missed Tessa during his incarceration, but he had missed his shop. He had begun learning how to tattoo when he had picked up the ink machine for the first time at sixteen. His natural talent for drawing had found a useful tool and had unfolded, merging with the ink machine until he had become known for the work he did. He had scraped enough cash together to open a small shop. It wasn't in the greatest area of town, yet he was where he needed to be to get the customers that wanted his tats.

It was the best choice he ever made and the worst. The clients and money had come in a steady supply, providing him with large sums of money for the first time in his life. It had also given Tessa access to those who would supply her with coke for her ever-increasing need. Colton had tried to put a stop to it when he found out, but was too late.

He found himself in prison after King had managed to

warn him in time that a drug bust was going down. Colton had succeeded in getting there just in time to pretend the buy was for him, which had earned Tessa a stint in rehab and him a five-year prison sentence. He would still be there if his parole hadn't been approved.

Technically, he owed King a favor, and unfortunately, King was not a man you wanted to owe favors to. Colton wouldn't feel truly free until the favor had been repaid.

The drive took over an hour and, by the time Tessa pulled up in front of the apartment King had rented for him, he felt like he was going to pull his hair out. Colton could only marvel at his stupidity for marrying Tessa; her voice was grating on his nerves so badly he wanted to yell at her to shut the fuck up.

Tessa started to get out of the car after pulling into an empty parking spot.

"Give me the key." Colton held out his hand for the keys to the apartment.

"I was..." Her voice turned seductive. It was obvious what she thought was going to transpire. It wasn't going to happen, though.

"Just tell me where the apartment is and I'll take it from here. I don't need you to hold my hand." Colton put an end to her maneuvering.

Tessa's lips tightened, but she still reached into her purse. "We have business to discuss."

"Nothing that we can't talk about in the morning when I show up at the shop," Colton said grimly, holding out his hand. Tessa placed two sets of keys and a cell phone in the palm of his hand.

"Apartment 3G." She pointed towards a large building. "Your bike is over there on the end. King had one of his boys bring it over this morning."

Colton didn't give her another word as he stepped out of the car. He was about to close the door when she told him what he already knew.

"King said rest a couple of hours then come and see

him." She couldn't even meet his eyes now.

Colton slammed the car door, not bothering to go up to the empty apartment. Instead, he went to his bike. Climbing on, he turned on the motor and listened for several seconds before backing it out of the parking space and turning his bike in the direction of King's bar. He was going to see King and get it out of the way. Once he found out what King wanted, he could put the mess of his life back in order.

Chapter One

"I want to see King," Colton told the bouncer standing in the doorway. The impassive bouncer talked into the headphone in his ear.

"Corner booth." Backing up, he let Colton through the doorway.

Colton could see that King had changed the décor since he was last there. The booths had been replaced with leather couches and tables, leaving one booth to remain in the room; the one in the back corner.

Passing through a maze of tables, he ignored the faces of King's customers, all focused on the stripper dancing on the stage. Colton kept his eyes from her. As soon as he left here, he would make a few phone calls until he found a woman willing to take care of the need driving his body. Colton, who had begun having sex when he was thirteen and had a ready supply by the time he was sixteen, had just suffered through the last three years with nothing. It had been torturous.

"King." Colton stood in front of the table, facing the man who had helped him save Tessa from jail time. He wasn't looking forward to paying back the favor. King had waited three years for his repayment; fucker wasn't even giving him a day of freedom before calling in his marker.

"Colton, have a seat." King sat with a whiskey in front of him. "You look good. I thought you would look half-starved."

He had actually gained a few pounds in prison, using his free time to work out and sculpt his lean frame into pure muscle.

"I heard you didn't have too hard of a time," King queried.

"You know I didn't. You kept me loaded on the commissary so I could trade for shit. Even heard that you put out the word not to touch me." Colton let King know he was aware of how big a debt he owed.

King shrugged, neither admitting nor denying the rumor.

"What do you want King?" Colton decided to come to the point.

King's eyes narrowed as he leaned back in the booth. "I need you to watch over a woman for me."

"Why do you need me to do that? You have enough men working for you that are more capable than me," Colton looked pointedly around the room at King's men. Hell, the bouncer at the door would be the only protection anyone would need.

"It's the dancer on the stage."

Colton's eyes reluctantly went to the stage. Under the lights he saw a brunette woman that had him gripping the table. She was fucking gorgeous with her long, shapely legs and perfect breasts under the see-through, black, flimsy dress that stopped at the top of her thighs. The dress was completely sheer, allowing every man in the room to see her luscious breasts. A tiny black patch over her pussy was the only thing hidden from view. She turned her back to the audience, showing an ass that made his already hardening cock thicken behind his jeans.

"Who the fuck is that?" Colton could already envision

himself driving his dick into her pussy while those long legs wrapped around his waist.

"That is Vida, she's Goldie's daughter."

Colton's cock deflated. "Fuck." She was younger than she looked on the stage. The lights and heavy make-up made her appear older.

King took a drink of his whiskey, satisfied with his reaction.

"She old enough to be working for you?" Colton questioned.

"She's twenty-three; a senior at WLU, getting a computer science degree."

"Why is she working for you? To pay her tuition?" Colton asked in disgust. Not for the young girl, but towards King for hiring her.

King's lips thinned further, his hand tightening on his glass.

"Watch yourself, Colton. I'm giving you a certain amount of leeway because I want you to do this favor for me, but as you said yourself, I do have other options."

Colton bit back his retort. "What is she shaking her titties for then? I would think that even you wouldn't want Goldie's daughter on that stage. She would turn over in her grave if she knew her kid was working for you."

"I agree. That's where you come in. I can only offer a certain amount of protection when she's not at the club. When she is here, I can't show favoritism among the women. She is expected to perform the same jobs as the other women. If you take her, then she will be safe without having to use me as protection and as you said, stop shaking her titties."

Fuck, Colton looked back toward the stage at the young woman dancing. She looked like her mother except for the hair. The natural sultriness that she had seemed to inherit in spades was driving the men nuts. Goldie had been one of King's strippers when he had first started in the business. Colton had been a randy twenty-year-old when he had seen her on the stage. There hadn't been a man breathing who could look at Goldie and not want her, she had been that gorgeous. She had earned her stage name because she had a heart of gold. Anyone who said that strippers were cold-hearted had never met Goldie. It was a fucking shame her daughter was on that stage.

King and Goldie had grown up together. Colton, who had also grown up in the same poor neighborhood, had at first thought that King was in love with Goldie, but quickly realized his assumption was wrong when Goldie started stripping. King was just beginning his rise to power, but he was a possessive bastard. If Goldie had been his, she would never have been stripping for money.

"Who are you protecting her from?" Colton asked curiously.

King took another drink of his whiskey before replying, "Digger."

"Fuck." Digger ran the biggest prostitution ring in the country. His girls serviced the higher-end clients— everyone from movie stars to rocks stars—but when they were done, the girls disappeared for good. Colton was sure they were sold off to some pervert.

King ran a clean house, while Digger didn't care; often keeping the women addicted to drugs to keep them in line. The police couldn't catch the slimy bastard, yet they had managed to lock him away for a relatively minor score. Fucking justice.

"Yeah, he managed to get his hands on a friend of hers and he plans to keep her. I need to find something he wants more than her. Until I do, he isn't too happy with Vida for going to the cops. He will either try to snatch her or shut her up. Either way, Vida is going to be in a world of pain."

Colton agreed. Dammit, if it had been anyone else, Colton would have done it without hesitation and enjoyed himself in the process. Taking another look at Vida and her fucking long legs tore at his conscience. No way could he bring himself to touch her. Having just got out of prison, he was about to explode he wanted a woman underneath him so badly, but now he was going to have this young girl in close proximity until King could find a way to help her friend.

"Who's the friend?" Sick to his gut, he already knew before the name passed King's tight lips.

"Sawyer."

Everyone in the neighborhood would often see the girls playing together when they were younger, growing closer as they grew older. His mother had lived in the same neighborhood as the girls so, when he visited his mother, he would often see them outside.

The building his mother had lived in had been marginally better than some of the others, but the one the girls had lived in had been the worst. He had hardly ever been there between work and play, yet no one could miss the little girls playing on the playground, their giggles always drawing attention. Sawyer, Vida and Callie drove everyone crazy with their escapades, getting away with their antics many times without their mothers' knowledge. Even now, Colton smiled, remembering a few of the stories his mother had told him.

"You going to help me out?"

"Do I have a choice?" Colton asked, his voice tight.

"Not if you want to consider your debt paid," King answered with a raised brow.

"Then it seems I have a new roommate," Colton said, watching Vida approach their table.

* * *

The lights are bright tonight, Vida thought. King must have had one of his men change the bulbs. She went down in a squat with the pole between her legs and the men's yells increased. Blanking their voices from her mind, she wished she had taken one of the pills that Sherri had promised would relax her, but Vida was determined not to fall down that road. She had enough problems without adding drugs to the mix.

Coming to her feet and dancing to the edge of the stage, she came close enough for the men to begin putting cash in the string that went around her waist. At least he allowed her to cover her front, leaving her ass and breasts exposed.

The fingers that shoved a twenty into her string tried to grab her ass, but Vida shimmied over to the next man who was waiting with a twenty. In the bright lights, she tried to make out the ones holding the larger denomination bills, going to them and bending down in a squat for them to put the bills on her. She had learned within the first two days to not look at the faces, to just stare at the money. It gave her enough strength to make it to the next man waiting his turn.

Thankfully, Vida heard her music come to an end. Standing up and hating what she was about to do, she gave her breasts an extra jiggle before turning and exiting the stage.

Sherri was up next, waiting behind the curtain in a silky pink robe. Her music started the second Vida disappeared behind the curtain.

"King wants to see you before you get changed."

"Thanks." Vida swallowed hard. She had hoped to get done on time today. She needed to get some lab time in before the grades were due otherwise, unless she had twenty hours logged lab time, she wouldn't get a grade.

Vida went outside to the bar area, making her way to the booth at the back of the room. She had noticed when she had come out to dance that he was sitting in his private booth. King sat there every night during the first few shows, judging the women's routines, surveying the crowds and removing customers who didn't obey the rules of his club.

She was sick to her stomach to have to talk to him.

He controlled everything within the city, moving between the spoiled world of the rich and entitled to the dregs of human society who had long ago lost their morals. He earned money legally through his clubs and illegally through gambling and prostitution.

 She had met him a couple of times when her mother was unable to find a sitter. He would hide her in a back room during her mother's show. Even as a child she had recognized the fear everyone had in their eyes when he was near. However, he had been her only recourse when her friend, Sawyer, disappeared a month ago.

Sawyer had been working as a waitress in a restaurant downtown when she met Rick Redman and began dating him. Vida still remembered her getting ready to go out for the evening in a new dress and freshly done nails. Vida, sharing an apartment with Sawyer, had been skeptical of the over-groomed businessman's interest in Sawyer when he had picked her up that night. When she didn't return, her skepticism turned to downright fear.

Worried sick, Vida had gone to the police. They put out a missing persons report, but it had been of little help—Sawyer had no family or friends other than Vida. Vida, not receiving encouraging answers from the police, had turned to King for help. Within twenty-four hours, King discovered information that had terrified Vida.

Rick Redman was not the concert promoter he had told Sawyer he was. The bastard was a pimp for high-class call girls. Vida had sunk to the floor when King had told her, envisioning Sawyer drugged, raped and held captive against her will.

She had begged King for help and he had agreed to help, but for a price. Vida would move into his club where he could keep an eye on her while he would try to get Sawyer back. He had warned her it would take some time since he needed to find out who Redman worked for.

Vida had wanted to refuse, yet she had known King was her only chance after she had gone to the police and they couldn't find a trace of Redman. Vida's options were few; either go to work for King or lose her childhood friend forever. Vida began stripping three nights later after King's women had given her a crash course in seductively taking her clothes off under the black lights.

Her knees were trembling as she crossed the large dim room. As she came closer, she noticed King wasn't alone. Vida hadn't seen the man in the club before. His disconcerting gaze made her want to run back to the dressing room, however King's frown pulled her forward.

"Sherri said you wanted to talk to me?" She trained her gaze on King.

"I want you to get your bags packed; you're going with Colton. He's a friend of mine that I trust will keep you safe. After your current two-week schedule is up, I'll take you off permanently. Staying with Colton will provide a reasonable excuse of why you're no longer stripping.

"But how am I going to pay you back?" Vida protested.

King shrugged. "You have already made me a nice chunk of change. Two more weeks of your dancing and six scheduled lap dances should cover my costs."

Vida swallowed. The dancing made her sick to her stomach, but the lap dances were the worst; she had to become physically close to the men. King charged the men twice the usual cost of his other girls, but they still chose Vida if she was there.

"I'll pack my bag." Vida cast a look at the stone-faced man before turning away, happy to be leaving the club, yet reluctant to stay with King's friend. She was unhappily aware she had no choice in the matter, though.

* * *

"Make sure you have her here for her shifts." King took a drink of his whiskey. "You sure you don't want one of the girls to give you some relief before you leave?"

Colton shook his head, almost instantly regretting his decision. He was going to be living with a beautiful woman that was off limits and he hadn't had one in three years.

It was a mindfuck that he didn't need or want.

Chapter Two

Vida watched as Colton unlocked the door to his apartment. She was still trembling from the ride from King's club. She had never ridden on a motorcycle before and his snapped, "Hold on tight", had startled her when she had gingerly put her arms around his waist.

Colton put her bag down by the door. He then moved through the apartment, opening and shutting doors before coming back and picking up her bag.

"There's only one bedroom and since I've only slept on a twin bed for the last three years, you can take the couch."

"I can sleep on the couch." Vida would sleep on the floor as long as it was outside of the Purple Pussycat. The club had four bedrooms and each one was shared by three women. If one of the women she was sharing a room with decided to have company and there were no private rooms available, she would bring her guest back to the shared bedroom. Vida had walked into several situations that had been too embarrassing for words before she could tactfully leave the room.

Colton threw her a thoughtful look before putting her bag on the chair. "There is a hall closet; you can stash your stuff there. You hungry?"

"No, I already ate."

"I have to go out. If you get hungry, there's supposed to be food in the cabinets and fridge."

"Okay." Vida went to the chair, picked up her backpack and began pulling out her schoolbook and laptop. Going to the small kitchen table, she organized everything she would need before sitting down.

Vida felt Colton's sharp gaze touch on her briefly before leaving the room. She took a deep breath once he'd left.

His presence was overwhelming. His height alone was intimidating without his fierce expression. He didn't come out and say she was an inconvenience to him, but from his abrupt voice and mannerisms, she could tell he was pissed. Vida had little doubt that he was as much under King's thumb as she was herself.

He was uptight about something and Vida could tell by his vibes he was anxious to be away from her. The sound of the shower running put Vida's mind to imagining him without his clothes. She could picture his hard body with water sliding over his flesh.

Determined to change the direction of her thoughts, Vida opened her book and then powered up her laptop, focusing on doing her homework. If she wasn't careful, she could easily get behind. She didn't have much longer; only another month and she would have the diploma she had worked so hard for.

Vida looked up from her book when Colton emerged from the bedroom. His hair was still wet and he was wearing a faded pair of jeans and a black t-shirt. He moved quietly, even while wearing heavy motorcycle boots. She swallowed nervously, her eyes dropping back to her book.

"I have to go out for a couple of hours. Lock the door behind me and don't answer it for anyone. Have you got a cell phone?"

Vida picked up her cell phone lying beside the

computer.

"Let me have it." She was becoming aware Colton had issues with politeness.

Vida handed him her cell phone, watching as he looked it over, then with a series of movements he handed it back to her.

"I programmed my number into it. Call me immediately if there's a problem." His face was expressionless as Vida nodded her head, not knowing what else to say. She was a nervous wreck being in the same room with him.

She had, until lately, been with young men her own age and had never considered herself shy, yet the last two weeks working at the strip club where men thought she was readily available for their amusement, had changed her. She had quickly learned to become cautious around men.

Colton was different; she'd seen it in his eyes. He had seen her naked and wasn't interested. Feelings of shame almost overwhelmed her, but she quickly squashed them and reached for her pencil, making notes on her assignment page.

She felt him hesitate before leaving and then the door closed softly behind him. Vida got up; making sure the door was locked then went back to her homework while refusing to allow her thoughts to wander to where Colton was going at this time of night.

* * *

A knock sounded on the door just as Colton was about to reach for Rae again.

"You expecting someone?" Colton asked, reaching for his pants instead.

"No. Don't get dressed. I'll see who it is and get rid of them," Rae protested as she watched him cover his taut ass with his jeans before zipping them closed.

"Answer the door." Colton didn't stop getting dressed, pulling his t-shirt over his head as Rae shrugged on a bathrobe. He had just finished putting on his boots when she returned.

"He says he has a message from King." Rae had fear in her eyes. Colton got to his feet and went into Rae's living room where one of King's men stood by the door waiting. His impassive face watched as Rae leaned against him as if seeking protection.

"King wants a talk. He's outside." Giving the message, he remained still, waiting for Colton's reply.

"I'm on my way." A sharp nod and the man left, leaving the door open. Colton took the hint that King meant now.

"I have to go, Rae. It was good seeing you again." Colton pulled the woman he had known for several years close, giving her a quick kiss before turning towards the door.

"You're not coming back?" Colton could hear the disappointment in her voice.

"Not tonight. I'll give you a call."

Without giving her a chance to reply, he left, closing the door behind him. He would call, just not too soon. He had no intention of giving her a reason to believe he wanted anything except a fuck. He had finally got out of prison and he was going to make damn sure that this time he remained emotionally free from a woman. He wasn't about to let another one get a hold over him, ever again.

Taking his time, he spotted King's ride in the parking lot and walked toward the car. The back door opened as he approached. Sliding in, he was met by an angry King glaring at him through the hazy smoke of his lit cigarette.

"Tell me why, when I gave you the job of watching Vida, you're here fucking? Leaving her alone is not protecting her," King said sarcastically.

"Because I have been locked up for three years and I needed to fuck before I lost my mind holed up with her," Colton replied just as sarcastically.

"I offered one of the women before you left," King

snapped.

"I didn't want paid-for pussy. I wanted a woman who wanted a fuck, not someone who was only in it because she works for you."

King stiffened. "All the women who work for me want to work. I don't force any of them to do what they don't want."

"Did Vida want to take off her clothes?" Colton returned his sarcasm.

King threw his cigarette out the window. "I gave her the choice. She was smart enough to know it was actually safer for her to blend in with the rest of the women."

"Doesn't matter. I'm finished here."

"Colton." King's voice stopped him before he could get out of the car. "Anything happens to that girl on your watch, I won't be happy." He left little doubt how unhappy he would be, so Colton simply nodded, getting out of the car.

* * *

Vida heard the keys in the door and pretended to be asleep on the couch. He fumbled with the latch on the door after closing it, his footsteps quiet as he crossed the room. The sound of the door to his room opening and closing allowed the tension to ease from her stiff body. Rolling to her side, Vida closed her eyes, feeling safe for the first time in a long time.

Chapter Three

The smell of frying bacon woke Colton. He hadn't smelled the delicious aroma for the last three years. Stretching out in the comfortable bed, Colton felt a moment's guilt for taking the bed and making Vida sleep on the couch. The memory of the short length of the couch squashed his remorse quickly, though.

He momentarily thought about finding another apartment that would give them more room, but King had promised the girl wouldn't be with him long. Rising from the bed, he walked naked to the shower, anxious to get to the tattoo shop. He had missed the shop more than he had any one person and he wanted to get there early enough to check everything out before everyone started arriving for the day.

Vida fixed herself a plate of food then sat at the table, almost choking on the toast when Colton came out of his room. The man seriously made her nervous.

"Did you save any for me?" Colton stared at the massive plate of food before her.

"There's plenty on the stove," Vida answered when her mouth was empty.

Colton fixed himself a plate and then sat at the table across from her. Vida watched him eat from underneath her lashes.

"You don't talk much, do you?"

"It's hard to talk to someone you don't know very well," Vida answered him as she fiddled with her food. She felt herself turning red at his direct question. She couldn't understand how she'd managed to get on a stage and strip naked when a simple question from him embarrassed her.

"I'm going into the shop this morning and, since I'm supposed to keep an eye on you, that means you're going, too," Colton informed her.

"I can't," Vida answered, looking up from her plate. "I have class in an hour then a lab. I can come to the shop afterward."

"That won't work. I'm not babysitting you while I have work to do." Colton stared at Vida as her whole countenance changed. She went from a shy, young woman to boldly direct.

"I don't care. I only have two weeks of classes left. If I miss any more classes, I'll flunk. I graduate this semester and I'm not going to flunk out." Vida's determined voice left Colton no doubt he would have to make other arrangements.

"What did King do about your classes?"

"He sent Henry with me. He would wait outside during my classes," Vida answered his question.

"I'm not blowing half my day sitting on my ass." Taking out his cell phone, he called King. Vida hoped King had another option because she wasn't missing class.

Vida cleaned the dishes as she listened to him argue with King until Colton ended the phone call abruptly. "King is going to send Henry for you. He'll stay with you until you're done then bring you to my shop."

Vida smiled, relieved that she wouldn't have to miss class.

Colton's eyes narrowed on the attractive woman, reminding himself that she was much younger than him and was also Goldie's daughter. *This situation isn't going to last long,* Colton kept reminding himself.

Vida turned back to the sink, finishing the dishes as Colton continued to eat his breakfast. She had just finished when she heard a knock at the door. Quickly, she dried her hands and grabbed her backpack as Colton answered the door to Henry.

"Hi, Henry, how's it shaking?" Vida joked with the burly man.

Henry smiled and Vida returned it with a smile of her own, both ignoring Colton as they turned to leave.

"What time do you get finished? I have some errands that need to be taken care of today and I don't want another visit from King for not keeping track of you."

Henry answered for her. "I'll feed her lunch then drop her off at your shop around one."

Colton nodded, watching as they disappeared down the apartment staircase before getting his bike keys and leaving the apartment. They had already left the parking lot by the time he got there. As he climbed on his bike, he took a deep breath of air. He didn't think he would ever again take his freedom for granted.

Throttling his bike, Colton put Vida and King out of his mind as he headed to his shop.

* * *

As Vida came out of class, she saw Henry leaning on the door of the expensive car.

"Ready?" Henry asked.

"Yes, I'm finished for the day." He held the car door open for her as she climbed inside the luxurious car.

Vida sat quietly in the backseat as Henry drove through the city. It wasn't long before he pulled up in front of a brightly painted tattoo shop with the name Green Dragon Tats. The dragon claws looked like needles.

She sat, hesitating to get out of the car until Henry

opened the door. "Come on, Vida; it'll be fine."

Vida liked Henry. As King's main bouncer, a lot of the women threw themselves at him to get closer to King. Henry found it amusing that Vida went the completely opposite route of using him to avoid contact with King. Both Henry and Sherri had become unexpected friends since she had begun stripping.

"Can't I just go back to the apartment and wait there? I promise not to go anywhere." Vida really didn't want to spend the rest of the day in Colton's grumpy presence.

"You know King won't be happy with that, Vida." Henry was her friend, but King's orders would always come first.

Vida sighed, getting out of the car. Henry watched her go into the shop before pulling out.

When she opened the tattoo shop door to find the front lobby empty, she waited hesitantly by the door for several minutes before a tall, leggy blond came out. Vida felt like a brown mouse next to the extremely attractive woman. She had a natural sexiness that Vida had to work to bring into her act and was only able to maintain for minutes at a time.

"Can I help you?" The woman pasted a polite, plastic smile on her face, waiting for Vida to answer her question.

"I'm supposed to meet Colton here." Vida made her voice firm, not wanting the woman to know she was nervous.

Her eyes narrowed and the plastic smile vanished. "I'm sorry, but Colton isn't taking any appointments today. Call back later in the week and I'll schedule you with someone—"

"That's enough, Tessa. Vida isn't here for a tattoo. I hired her to watch the front desk."

Tessa rounded on Colton as he came into the lobby. "We don't need one of your whores sitting on her ass behind the desk. I did fine without having someone sitting here all the time while you were gone."

"It doesn't matter what you want, Tessa, it's what I want that matters. You don't like it, go work for another shop."

"Fine, she can stay, but her paycheck comes from your share of the profits," Tessa snapped back her response.

Vida watched the exchange between the two, turning red as Tessa cast her a venomous look before turning and leaving the room. Colton pulled out the chair from behind the desk.

"Make yourself useful." Vida came to stand behind the counter. "If someone calls, make an appointment for them. Here are the names of the artists available, rotate them out so that the customers are evenly spaced. If someone requests a certain artist, fulfill their request if possible, but try not to overload any particular artist."

Vida nodded her head.

"Any questions?" Colton asked.

"I don't think so, it seems pretty simple," Vida answered, looking over the appointment book.

"It is. If you need anything, just yell. I need to get back to my room." Colton walked away.

Vida sat down in the chair, studying the appointment book as she familiarized herself with the artist's names. The phone began ringing and for the next several minutes, Vida made appointments. When the phone finally quieted, she opened her backpack and took out her laptop. Vida quickly became engrossed with her homework, only lifting her head when she heard the bell over the door ring.

A tall, gangly young man approached the counter with a hesitant smile.

"I was wondering if it would be possible to get a tattoo. I don't have an appointment."

Vida searched through the appointment book. "I have an opening in twenty minutes if you want to wait?"

"Sounds good."

"What's your name?"

"Seth Redman." Vida wrote his name down in the

appointment book.

Giving her a friendly grin, he leaned on the counter. "You into computers?" he asked, motioning toward her laptop.

"Yes, I'm almost finished with my degree in computer science," Vida replied.

"I do I.T. for the local hospital."

"That sounds interesting." Vida thought any job out in the workforce sounded interesting. She was tired of schoolwork and was eager to put what she had learned in school to use.

He made a face. "Nope, boring as hell. Wanted to design computer games, but those jobs are hard to come by, and I like to eat and get tattoos. Both cost money."

Vida laughed.

"I'm working on a game app. I don't suppose you have any free time to help me out with a few glitches?" Vida studied his face, seeing his hesitance in asking. He seemed like an awkwardly sweet guy. It was a nice change from her morose roommate.

"I think it sounds like fun, but I'm afraid I don't have much free time." Vida tore a piece of paper from her notebook and wrote down her phone number. Before she could change her mind, she handed it to him. As she handed Seth her number, Colton walked into the room with his eyes going straight to the slip of paper.

"He's waiting for either you or Reverend to give him a tattoo," Vida told him.

Colton nodded. "Have you decided what tattoo you want?"

Seth reached into his pocket, pulling out a piece of paper and handing it to Colton. They left the room, talking about the design. Vida returned to studying, relieved to have the lobby to herself once again.

Several more clients came in and Vida wrote down their names to work them into a rotation with the tattoo artists. Tessa came out once, taking a client that wanted a tattoo of a rose. She ignored Vida, merely checking off her name next to the client.

It didn't bother Vida that Tessa was being rude to her. It was obvious Tessa and Colton had a history as well as that her presence obviously had been sprung on Tessa without any warning or explanation.

Vida had no intention of becoming friendly with Colton. Maybe when Tessa realized she had no intentions towards him, her frosty demeanor would thaw.

Her mother had shown her the futility of trying to have a relationship with a man like Colton. The relationship would be intense at first then gradually his attention would wander to other available women. Vida wondered if that was what had happened between the two of them.

Vida stared blindly out the window, missing Sawyer, wishing she could call her and complain about everyone being assholes to her for no reason. It wasn't the first time in her life she had to adjust to losing a friend. She only hoped that she would be able to help Sawyer, unlike Callie.

She swallowed down the lump in her throat at the thought of Callie, relieved when a man covered in tattoos appeared from the back of the shop to divert her thoughts. When he leaned against the counter with a flirtatious smile on his good-looking face, Vida couldn't help but to return the smile he was throwing her way.

"Who are you, sweet thing?" He crooned.

Vida blushed at his accomplished flirting. "I'm Vida."

"I'm Reverend, but you can call me Rev," he said with soulful, chocolate eyes. "Where did you come from?"

"Colton hired me temporarily." Vida wasn't quite sure how to explain her presence behind the counter, so she stuck with the same explanation that Colton had given Tessa.

Rev's smile widened. "I was looking forward to having Colton back. Now I have him to thank for the prettiest woman to walk through that door in a while."

Tessa slammed a folder down in front of Vida, causing her to jump unexpectedly. She hadn't even been aware the woman had entered the room.

"Don't you have a client waiting?" she asked Reverend snidely, motioning to the man sitting quietly in the waiting room.

"Nope, he's all yours. I'm waiting on an appointment, and Colton is finishing up with his client."

Vida watched Tessa's lips tighten before she motioned to the waiting man to follow her into the back.

"It gets better and better. Anyone that pisses off that bitch is a friend of mine."

Vida hid her smile. Truthfully, Tessa's attitude didn't bother her. She had dealt with women with far worse attitudes than hers.

Rev's client came in and with a wave, he escorted him to his room. After that, the rest of the day passed quickly. Colton barely paid any attention to her as he came out for his clients, which meant that, other than Tessa's unfriendly attitude, it hadn't been a bad experience.

Vida yawned, closing her book and turning off her computer. Her eyes were burning with tiredness. The late nights at the club and the hours of studying were beginning to wear her down. Tonight was her off night from the club and she simply wanted to sink into the soft couch at Colton's apartment and catch up on her sleep.

Colton came into the room, carrying an extra helmet. "You ready?"

Vida nodded, putting her books and laptop into her backpack before rising to follow him out the door. Outside, he handed her the helmet before climbing on. Vida put on the helmet then shrugged into her backpack. Scrambling onto the bike, she gripped Colton's waist as he started the motor and pulled out of the parking lot.

As they entered the door to the apartment, Vida couldn't help eyeing the couch longingly.

"You know how to cook?" Vida was about to sit down

on the couch when his question stopped her.

"A little," Vida confessed reluctantly.

"Good, find us something to eat while I grab a shower." He walked away before she could tell him she wasn't hungry.

Her shoulders slumped as she took off her backpack then headed into the kitchen to find them something to eat. Colton didn't look back, going to his room to shower. It made Vida seriously tempted to stick out her tongue at his departure.

She opened the cabinets, searching through the contents before going to the refrigerator to see what was inside. Vida came to a decision quickly, opening a can of soup and making them a couple of sandwiches once she saw the bread on the counter.

She was pouring the soup into bowls when Colton returned to the small kitchen. "Smells good," he complimented.

"It's just sandwiches and soup." Vida hadn't lied; she wasn't much of a cook. She had never had an overabundance of food, and when money was scarce, you tended to buy only the basics.

Colton picked up his bowl and sandwich, carrying them to the table before going to the refrigerator to grab himself a beer.

"What do you want to drink?" He paused, waiting for her answer.

"A bottled water, thanks," Vida said as he put the bottle on the table. Reluctantly, Vida carried her food to the table, sitting down across from him. They ate quietly; Vida thinking about her classes for the next day while also trying to divert herself from thoughts of having to work at the strip club.

"Do you work tonight?" Vida's eyes rose from her half eaten sandwich.

"No, I'm off tonight. I work tomorrow from eight until two."

Colton took a drink of his beer, studying the young woman. He'd noticed the shadows in her clear green eyes when he had mentioned work. He had already begun to be aware that she was embarrassed to be working at the club. She blushed bright red anytime it was mentioned.

"How long have you been working for King?"

"A couple of weeks." Colton noticed her fingers begin to play with the soup spoon.

He attempted to mind his own business, however he couldn't prevent himself from speaking. "You could get out of town until King gets your friend back..."

Vida was already shaking her head. "I can't leave knowing Sawyer is in trouble and I could have helped her. I won't bury another friend of mine." She got up from the table and took their dishes to the sink. She found a sandwich bag in one of the drawers, placed her half eaten sandwich inside and then put it in the refrigerator.

"What are you doing?"

Looking at Colton, she saw his incredulous eyes on her. Not knowing what he meant, she paused. "What?"

"Why did you save that sandwich when there were only a couple of bites left?"

"I don't like to waste food. Later, when I get hungry, I'll finish it." Vida refused to be embarrassed about not wasting food.

"You could also have made yourself another one," Colton said through gritted teeth. "I think I can afford to feed you a couple of sandwiches. I might not have a lot of groceries, but I haven't been to the store myself. What food is in the cabinets was just put in there so I would have enough until I went to the grocery store myself."

Vida stared at him uncomprehending. "Why do you need to go to the store? Your cabinets and refrigerator are full."

Colton stopped what he had been about to say when realization hit him. Turning away, he took a long drink of his beer. Telling himself over and over in his mind he needed to mind his own fucking business. The more he learned about Vida, the more he would draw closer to her and he had no intentions of that happening.

She was too young, too sweet and in too much fucking trouble. Her mother would turn over in her grave to see the predicament that Vida was in. She had worked her ass off to make sure Vida didn't end up in the same situation as her, determined for a better life for her child.

Colton had known Goldie, hell, he had even partied with her a couple times after her sets, but they had only been friends. Even though she was a beautiful woman, the desire for her just hadn't been there, probably because she was so nice.

Dumb fuck that he was, he had always preferred women with a bitchy temperament. It had been his downfall, too; there was no bigger bitch than Tessa. He had also been well aware Goldie had a kid at home. He had damn sure not wanted to become entangled in a relationship where anything might be expected of him.

Colton had always been about covering his own ass. He had even thought that his relationship with Tessa had been under his control. The sneaky bitch had proven him wrong and the three-year prison term he had just finished proved he needed to take what he wanted from women and leave the emotional crap out of it.

The doorbell rang as Colton watched Vida wash the dishes. Glancing at his watch, it was exactly eight o'clock. She was right on time.

Vida paused in her chore of washing the dishes as Colton answered the door. A pretty, curvy blond entered the room as he held open the door. Then a loud squeal filled the room as the blond flung herself into Colton's arms.

"Colton, I missed you so bad." Vida couldn't help watching as the woman jumped up with the aid of Colton's hands on her ass to wrap her legs around his waist.

Burying her hands in his long hair, the woman jerked his head down to give him a voracious kiss.

They kissed for several minutes before Colton pulled his head back. "It's good to see you again, too, Tracy." The woman turned towards the sound of the running water and, seeing Vida by the sink, surprise lit her eyes.

"You didn't tell me when you called it was going to be a party." Tracy's eyes glided over Vida's body and had her taking a step back. "I'm glad to see prison didn't dampen the fire in that cock of yours."

Laughing, Colton playfully smacked her ass while she was still wrapped around his waist. "No party, it's just the two of us. Go on in the bedroom, I'll be there in a minute."

Vida tried to appear inconspicuous as Tracy's legs loosened from around his waist and, giving her a last, lustful look, she left Colton and Vida alone in the room together.

Dragging a hand through his tumbled hair, Colton appeared to hesitate a second, trying to find the appropriate words. Vida decided to cut to the quick of the matter.

"It's cool. After I finish the dishes I'm going to sleep. I have a long day tomorrow."

Colton's eyes bore into her. "I would have gone to her place, but King doesn't think it's safe for you to be left alone." It was the closest to an apology she was going to get.

Vida shrugged. "I don't want to disrupt your life anymore than I have, so it's no big deal. I had a male roommate my freshman year in college." Vida didn't tell him that Ty was gay; afterall, he had still been her roommate.

She saw the relief in his face. "Cool. We'll try not to bother you. See you in the morning."

"Goodnight." Vida turned back to the dishes, hearing another loud squeal when the bedroom door opened.

She finished the dishes and wiped down the counters before gathering her clothes to take a shower. Ignoring the female moans from the bedroom as she entered the bathroom, Vida turned on the shower, deciding to wash her hair before washing her body; it would briefly drown out those moans she was hearing through the thin walls.

When she was finished, she put on her pajamas and robe. Leaving the bathroom, she rushed down the short hallway as the bed banging against the wall started echoing through the apartment. Vida quickly made up the couch with the sheet and blanket she had set to the side before taking a shower. Turning out the light, she lay down, trying not to think about what was going on in the bedroom. A loud scream had her putting the pillow over her head, wishing she were anywhere other than here.

Her room at the strip club hadn't been much better. When the other bedrooms had been filled, the women she shared her room with would always invariably bring the men to their room. Sometimes they would wake her up to get her out of the room, yet sometimes they wouldn't care, merely ignoring her presence and getting to the business of getting the man off as quickly as possible so they themselves could go to bed.

Vida dozed off to sleep with the pillow still over her head. She was so exhausted by that point that she didn't wake during the middle of the night when a gentle hand removed the pillow, replacing it under her head. Nor did she waken when long fingers threaded through her silken hair, letting it fall softly against her soft cheek.

Chapter Four

"Here comes Trouble," the announcer spoke above the catcalls of the men in the room, their avid eyes searching the curtain for Vida's appearance. She felt her stomach clench as she moved from the cover of the curtain into the lights focused on the stage.

The sequins on her outfit caught the lights and reflected the flashes of light throughout the room, drawing even more attention to her figure. Vida swallowed down the bile rising in her throat, forcing herself to blank the present from her mind. Pasting an imaginary picture of Sawyer across her mind, Vida began to dance seductively on the stage. How her mother could have done this for years defied Vida's imagination.

Deep sadness engulfed her. She knew how, the love a mother had for her child. Vida knew her mother had become pregnant at fifteen and ran away from home to live with her seventeen-year-old boyfriend. Her father had stayed until she was six months old then took off, returning to his own parents' loving arms. He left Goldie behind; however, her mother's parents were not as understanding and no longer wanted to have anything to do with her or their grandchild.

Goldie, despite being so young, was smart enough to manage to get child support, but it was barely enough to keep a cheap roof over their heads and not enough for much else. Uneducated with a small child, it took time for Goldie to get her GED and once she had finally earned it, not many more jobs opened up than before. She would manage to get waitressing or bar positions, but they paid little and barely covered the bills.

Vida hadn't been a healthy child. The low-income housing building was filthy and damp, setting off allergies. In addition, she had a genetic gastric problem that required her to have several surgeries, which forced her mother to miss work. Fired from another job, Goldie had turned to stripping. She could still remember the nights her mom would have a good night and wake her up when she came home.

They would go to the grocery store late at night and fill the cart with groceries that they both knew would have to last a while. The cute cereals and confections that other kids took for granted were passed over for bread and peanut butter. Vida remembered well the days where that was all she had to eat and was aware that she didn't eat much better as a college student.

The change in music alerted Vida to the next set where she would start to remove her red camisole. Teasingly unfastening each button slowly, she moved closer to pervert row before backing away, giving them the subliminal promise that she would soon be theirs if they could merely catch her long enough. When all the buttons where undone, the music rose, building to the climax of her removing her top.

Thankfully, the music that started her next set was slower, allowing her to catch her breath. Moving towards the men, she allowed them to stuff their money into the string that circled her waist. Their fingers lingering as long as they thought was possible before one of King's men would make an appearance. It lasted several minutes, the music spaced out to give her time to work from one side of the stage to the other before she moved back to the center stage, reaching down to pick up her top, giving the men one last look at her shaking ass.

Vida walked slowly off the stage to the dwindling music and loud applause.

"Damn girl, you keep that up and King will set you up as a feature dancer in his other clubs," Sherri remarked, waiting for her own music to start.

"You look great tonight, is that a new outfit?" Vida ignored the comment about her working at other clubs.

Sherri brushed her hand against the leather chaps she wore and grinned. "Yep, I plan to make them have to run to the bathroom to jerk off."

Vida simply shook her head, laughing. Sherri was one of the few women who actually stripped because she loved the attention. It made her feel like a star for the short time she was on stage. She was a sweet, likeable woman that had taken the time to actually try to get to know her and Vida couldn't help responding to her natural friendliness.

"Is King out front?" Vida asked.

"I think so. I saw him there a few minutes ago."

Sherri's music queued. "Don't break a leg," Vida warned her when she saw her outrageously high-heeled cowboy boots.

Sherri grinned at her as she moved toward the stage.

Vida went to the dressing room and put on her robe. She brushed her hair back down until it lay flat; her dancing had turned it into a tangled mess. The other women in the room ignored her, busy getting ready for their own sets.

Vida went in search of King, finding him sitting in his booth watching a customer give the shot girl a hard time. His facial expression did not change as he saw Vida approach.

"King, may I talk with you?"

"Have a seat, Vida. I was about to send Henry for you."

Vida slid into the booth across from him. He was, as always, dressed in an expensive, dark suit that made him appear even more intimidating. King put off menacing vibes which the dark suit only enforced.

"Have you found anything out about Sawyer yet?"

"As a matter of fact, I found her." His lips tightened into a grim line.

"You have?" Vida couldn't prevent the excitement from her face.

"Calm down, Vida. It's not the best situation, but for now she's safe. Rick Redman works for Digger." King paused, waiting for her reaction. It wasn't long in coming. Everyone in town knew Digger, he was as ruthless as King. The difference was King didn't attempt to hurt you as long as you didn't fuck with him. Digger liked to fuck you up for fun.

"One of the men that Digger sold her to for the night has decided to keep her for a while. As long as he pays for her company, Digger will remain content. For a while."

Disappointment filled Vida. She had accomplished nothing, she hadn't been able to keep Sawyer from being sold and used. Pain filled her expression as she felt the fruitlessness of her attempts sink in.

"Vida, she's not on the street, nor has she disappeared never to be seen again. Digger knows that, if she disappears, I'll kill him. Right now, he's trying to push my buttons, but not set me on a path of retaliation. As soon as I find out his price, you'll get her back." Vida listened as King tried to explain the intricacies of dealing with someone as dirty as Digger.

She nodded her head. "His henchman, Briggs, comes in the club sometimes. I could try to find out some information from him."

A cold glare was her answer. "Stay away from Briggs, he's Digger's enforcer. Let me handle it, Vida."

"Okay." Vida started to slide out of the booth.

"Where's Colton tonight?" King asked coldly, his eyes searching the room.

"Back at his place. He dropped me off and asked if Henry would give me a ride home."

"Quite the gentleman, isn't he?" he said sarcastically.

Vida shrugged. "I think I'm cramping his style; being in the way all the time."

"If anything happens to you, his style is going to be a little more than cramped," King threatened.

"Leave him alone, King, he's being really nice letting me stay at his place. I don't need him with me when Henry is here," Vida tried to reason with King.

King nodded his head reluctantly. "I'll tell Henry to walk you to your door."

"Thanks, King, for everything." She reached across the table and grabbed his hand, giving it a tight squeeze.

"Don't thank me yet," he replied grimly.

Vida simply smiled as she stood. It was time for her turn in the VIP room. The woman she was replacing would be angry if she was late. As she walked up the steps to the upper floor, she felt the men in the room watching. Several would also pay to go up to the room knowing she was on duty. Vida squashed down the butterflies in her stomach; this was worse than actually stripping on stage. For each minute the men paid for, she had to actually act like she wanted them, which made them want to purchase more dances.

The next hour passed swiftly as she served drinks and fulfilled two requests for lap dances. Vida's eyes widened when she noticed Briggs enter the room. He was always trying to find out what he could from the girls about King. King didn't mind, Briggs always spent a lot of money and King's staff was loyal. Moving forward, she decided tonight was going to be different. She was going to attempt to turn the tables on him and try to find out something they could use against Digger.

King would be furious, yet if she was careful, maybe he wouldn't find out. She would sneak the tip money from the lap dance to the other two women in the VIP room if they kept their mouths shut.

Sauntering within his eyesight, she brought him the drink he had requested from Angel. His eyes widened and his mouth parted when she bent low enough to allow him to see the pale globes of her breasts almost spill out of the red camisole.

"Can I get you anything else?" Vida murmured seductively, moving closer so that her perfume would surround him.

"Yeah, you can join me for a drink," Briggs said, not taking his eyes off her breasts. Vida sat down close to him on the couch. Catching his eyes with hers, she paid him all the attention he wanted, giving only monosyllabic replies when he tried to question about herself and King.

Catching Angel's eyes, she motioned for her to keep Briggs's drinks coming.

When his sweaty palm covered her stocking covered thigh, Vida sighed to herself; the next hour was shaping up to be one of the most difficult of her life.

* * *

Colton held the door open for Wanda to leave, motioning for her to be quiet. With a quick kiss, she went through the door. He shut and locked it behind her, turning to go into the kitchen. Seeing the pillow on top of Vida's face, he was determined not to remove it this time, however he found his legs moving towards her anyway.

Lifting the pillow, he saw tears glistening on her face and touching the pillow he found it damp. He had given her a key, not even noticing when she had returned. Turning the pillow over until the dry side was up, he laid her head back down on it. Brushing her tears away with the pad of his thumb, he stroked her soft cheek. Her face turned away, moving away from the soft touch.

Colton studied the dark circles of weariness underneath

her eyes. Vida, he had caught on early, actually slept very little, always staying busy with her computer or studying the books she carried around in her backpack.

She was unusual for a girl her age, so quiet and studious. Even when the customers tried to talk to her at the tattoo shop, she rarely engaged them back. Seth, the boy she had given her number to, had returned to the shop to work on coding with her. She was friendly to him, but he could see she kept a distance with them all. She had been staying with him for two weeks now and he had yet to see a genuine smile.

What was so surprising to him was that her mother, Goldie, had been full of life and laughter. She had worshipped her daughter and had been proud of her every achievement. It was hard to see her daughter completely full of restraint and wariness.

Colton was sure the death of Goldie two years ago had been extremely hard on her. Now her closest friend since childhood was in trouble. He knew it was probably weighing her down that she couldn't help Sawyer, just as she hadn't been able to help the friend who'd died. Goldie had often worried how losing such a close friend at a young age would affect her. Callie, Sawyer and Vida were the little troublemakers of the neighborhood. Now, only one was left.

Baring her body and doing the lap dances went against the repressed personality he saw in Vida. Emotionally, he wondered how she had remained so strong.

Turning away, he went to the kitchen to get a bottled water and looked at the clock on the microwave, seeing that it was almost four a.m. Finishing the water, he returned to the bedroom, lying back down on the rumpled sheets.

He had no problem filling his bed each night with a different woman, the tattoo shop and past pick-ups provided a steady flow to satisfy the hunger that had gone unfed the three years in prison. The only problem was he felt emptier and emptier with each additional encounter. Something was wrong and Colton was deathly afraid he knew what it was.

Placing an arm over his eyes, he tried to shut out the image of Vida from that first day he had been released from prison. He needed to get rid of her. Tomorrow night, instead of dropping her off at the club, he planned to go inside and have a talk with King. Vida had to go and King had to do something about it, regardless of the situation with Digger.

Chapter Five

Vida stood nervously behind the curtain in her red camisole and underwear. She only had the two outfits; one red and one black. The other women raised scornful eyes when they saw her dressed in the same outfit night after night, however she refused to invest in new outfits with only two more nights to go.

Hearing her queue, she went out on the stage and began her standard set.

* * *

Colton stood in the shadows in the back of the room as he watched Vida come onto the stage. Her perfectly proportioned body was highlighted by the high cut of her underwear and showed her legs to their best advantage. The tiny piece of red material barely covered her pussy, while leaving her creamy ass bare, the string disappearing between the luscious globes.

Colton battled his cock, trying to keep himself from getting hard, but it was an impossible feat as Vida's next set began and she started removing her top. Her seductive twisting was arousing; not only to him, but every man in the room. She slowly unbuttoned the flimsy camisole that hid her breasts, drawing out the tension in the men, denying them while at the same time providing tantalizing glimpses. When she could delay it no longer, the top was dropped, showing her full breasts in all their glory. The pink tipped nipples were hard from the air conditioning vent that was directed at her body, making her appear to want the men's lustful leers.

His hands clenched into fists as he heard some of the men's shouts, studying their faces so he could have a word with them later. Then Vida's music changed and she moved towards the men in the front row

She allowed their greedy hands to shove money into the thin string that barely held her thong on while she squatted in front of their faces. He was sure several of the men tugged on it harder than necessary, trying to break the tiny piece of material. Rising, she danced away from the front of the stage while the men begged her to come back. The music drew to an end, reaching the point where she bent down towards the floor to pick up her top, giving the men their money's worth by showing them her ass as she waved goodbye between her legs. Colton wanted to storm the stage and smack her ass hard.

A moment later, Henry motioned Colton forward, letting him know that King was finally ready to talk to him. As he moved towards the dark booth, Colton was surprised the light over it was turned off. Usually, when King was occupying the booth, the light was on. Now it was shrouded in darkness, giving complete privacy.

Colton took a seat across from him, watching as King leaned back against the expensive leather of the booth.

"Henry said you wanted to talk to me?"

"How much longer is this going to go on, King? I have a life—" Colton began.

King cut him off. "Which watching over Vida hasn't hindered in the least. You've had a different woman over every night, and other than a few hours of watching her at your shop and at night after she gets done here, you haven't been inconvenienced at all."

Colton refused to feel guilty. "She's complaining to you that I have women over?"

King showed his dangerous smile. "You've lived with her for two weeks and you don't know her better than that?" King shook his head. "You're a dumb son of a bitch. Tessa leads you around by the fucking nose and you believed every fucking lie she told you. Vida wouldn't open her mouth about you because she wouldn't want to jeopardize Sawyer's life. You need to learn the difference between an immoral bitch and a woman who's like her mother and has a heart of gold."

Colton stiffened in his seat. "I don't care what kind of woman she is, I want her gone."

King studied him. "Give me to the end of the weekend and I will make other arrangements."

Relief flooded through Colton, but before he could stop himself, he asked, "What kind of arrangements?"

King shrugged. "One of Margie's girls is leaving. One of her customers wants her full-time, so Vida can have her room and Margie can watch over her.

Anger flooded Colton. "Margie will fucking put her to work."

"What do you care, Colton? At least Margie will keep her safe and give her back when I get all this shit cleaned up. If Digger gets her, she'll either be dead or disappear."

Colton bit back his anger, smart enough to know if he pissed King off, he wouldn't leave the choice in his hands. "I'll let her stay. Just hurry it up, King."

"That was my intention all along." Satisfied, King motioned for the waitress to bring Colton a drink.

The waitress put a beer down in front of Colton, lingering by the table until King motioned her away. She left after a last smoldering look at Colton.

"Seems you have an admirer." Colton ignored him, watching Vida climb the steps to what Colton knew was the room that King had set aside for the private members.

"How many does she have scheduled for tonight?" Colton asked, nodding his head towards Vida.

"She's a popular little thing. She has three scheduled and several more will purchase one when they see her at work."

Colton gave King a hard look before taking his beer and getting up from the table, turning towards the stairway.

"There's a fee to go upstairs, Colton," King reminded him, trying to hide his amusement.

"Add it to my tab, asshole."

* * *

Vida finished giving a dance to one of the men who had become a regular and went to the bar for a drink of water before going into the side room to give another dance. Each dance lasted no more than ten minutes, but every time she felt as if she needed to take a shower to clean herself.

Vida glanced at the door when she heard it open, trying to hide the surprise on her face when Colton walked into the room. He cast her a hard look before taking a seat on one of the expensive couches. Finishing her water with trembling fingers, she put down her bottle before placing a seductive look on her face for her waiting customer. It was unnerving her that she felt Colton's dark eyes on her as she moved towards Briggs.

"Hey sexy, you ready?" Vida murmured.

His hot eyes ran over her body. Vida felt her skin crawl as his disgusting gaze slid over her. Carefully hiding her reaction, infusing fake warmness into her eyes, she held out her hand playfully for him to take. Briggs took her hand, rising to his feet and following her tamely into the private room where she would perform the lap dance.

Vida playfully pushed Briggs down onto the plush chair and backed away. The music started and Vida drew closer to Briggs, straddling his chair, grinding her corset-covered breasts against his chest. Twisting and turning her hips, she kept a distance of mere centimeters between her mound and his crotch.

Blushing in embarrassment, Vida fervently hoped that Colton hadn't turned so that he would be able to see into the room. It was semi-private due to a window so the bouncer would be able to watch and call a halt if one of the clients got out of hand.

King also provided completely private rooms, but Vida never went into those. It didn't take a genius to realize that more went on in there than lap dances. Usually the higher paid dancer's took advantage of those rooms.

The music sped up and Vida let her breasts lean more heavily onto Briggs's chest as she rubbed against him. Vida noticed sweat break out across his brow. A self-satisfied smile curled her lips and she let her bottom sink onto his lap, grinding her ass across his thighs.

"You're making me hard as a rock." Briggs's eyes stared lustfully into hers.

Vida swallowed down the bile in her throat and started silently counting in her mind to distract herself.

"Meet me after you get off tonight," he begged.

Vida shook her head, forcing herself to let more of her weight grind down on Briggs at the same time that a fake moan passed her lips. Taking a deep breath, she took her life in her hands.

"I don't trust you, Briggs. You work for Digger. I haven't seen Sawyer since his man took her out for a date." Vida let her voice go breathy.

"I didn't have anything to do with that, it was Rick. I'd take good care of you." Briggs's hands came up to cup her ass. Vida paused. "You know you're not allowed to touch," Vida scolded him.

Briggs immediately removed his hands and she felt his cock grow thicker under her. She subtly lifted her weight off him, using the beat of the music. Vida was sickened when she recognized that he had responded to the dominance in her voice.

She let her weight fall back down for the remaining minutes of the music. Briggs was grinding his teeth and Vida felt a spurt of satisfaction she couldn't repress. He wanted her. She was determined to use whatever means she had to get Sawyer back. The music ended and Vida pretended reluctance at getting off his lap.

"Come on, meet me tonight. Let's get into some trouble." Briggs thought he was being cute with his pun while Vida only thought he was pathetic.

Vida shook her head. "Maybe next time, Briggs. I'll have to think about it. Sawyer was my best friend and I miss her. I don't want to find myself in her shoes." Vida tried to appear frightened of him.

"Trouble, you're too fine. I'll take good care of you. I wouldn't let Digger touch you; he listens to me," he boasted, taking her arm in a hard grip.

"Really?" Pretending to think about it for a minute, she again shook her head. "Let me think about it, Briggs. I work next Friday. Will you come and see me dance?"

Briggs didn't try to hide his growing anger and Vida could tell she had pushed far enough for the night. She didn't try to pull her arm out of his grasp.

"Let me go," Vida demanded, trying to put just the right amount of dominance into her voice.

"I'll be here," Briggs said, reluctantly letting her arm go.

Blowing him a kiss, Vida slipped out of the door and walked into a hard wall of flesh. She looked up in surprise at the furious eyes staring down at her. Colton thrust her robe into her hand before taking her arm and leading her from the room. She almost fell trying to keep up with his angry strides.

"I can't leave, I have another customer."

"You're done for the night. I'm ready to leave. I told Henry to tell King to find a replacement for the end of your shift." Taking her to the doorway of the dressing room, he set her arm free.

"Get changed," he said stonily.

Vida wanted to leave, so she decided not to argue with him. She went into the dressing room and quickly changed into jeans and a long sleeved t-shirt. Grabbing her jacket, she headed back outside to a waiting Colton. He followed her outside into the crisp air, which felt wonderful to Vida after the stuffy confinement of the nightclub.

Handing her the helmet, Vida put it on and then climbed on behind Colton. Expecting to go back to his apartment, Vida was surprised when he pulled into a late night waffle house.

"I'm hungry; let's get something to eat," Colton said, getting off the bike.

Vida was never hungry after working at the club, but didn't say anything, merely going in with him and ordering a coffee when the waitress came.

"Bring her a stack of pancakes and some bacon," Colton ordered.

"But I'm not hungry," Vida protested.

"You've lost a good five pounds since you've been living with me. Your clothes are falling off of you. You're going to eat." Colton motioned the curious waitress away with a gesture of his hand after placing his own order.

Vida's lips tightened. She had been well aware of the weight she had lost, although she hadn't thought anyone else had noticed. She wasn't happy Colton was the one who'd paid that much attention. Hell, she thought he hadn't even been aware of what color her hair was the way he constantly ignored her.

"Now that my classes are over, my weight will come back. I've been overworked."

"Shaking your ass all over that stage and rubbing it against every man that has a hundred takes a lot of energy," Colton said snidely.

Vida stiffened in her chair. "Yes, well, I don't have much of a choice about that, do I?"

"You have a fucking choice; you just won't make the right one. Shake this town off and leave. King will

46

eventually get Sawyer back."

Vida stubbornly shook her head. She couldn't believe how he expected her to turn her back on Sawyer.

"I saw the game you were playing with Briggs. You're going to get yourself in more trouble than you can handle, Vida."

"I don't know what you're talking about." Vida looked out the restaurant window, avoiding his eyes.

"Yes, you do," Colton countered.

The waitress brought their food, setting it down in front of them. Vida took a bite of the warm, sticky pancakes and found herself starved, eating most of the plate without looking up. The waitress refilled her coffee and it was when she took a sip of the strong brew that she caught Colton's amused gaze on her.

Blushing, she looked at her almost empty plate with a smile. "I guess I was hungrier than I thought."

Laughing, Colton teased, "I see that, do you want me to order you another stack?" Vida couldn't help staring at the change in his face that the laughter had brought.

He was extremely good looking; his long, dark hair was tousled from the wind, giving him an untamed appearance while the metal ball that pierced his sensual bottom lip caused Vida to lower her gaze to his mouth. Reverend had talked him into it last week. Vida had almost died laughing when Rev had also offered to pierce his cock and Colton had told him where to stick his needles.

Vida could understand why he didn't have any trouble getting women in his bed. He was a woman's fantasy with the sexual vibes emanating from him. In fact, several women in the restaurant were constantly looking at their table. Even the waitress kept making frequent trips back to their table, brushing against him unnecessarily every time she refilled his coffee cup.

"Are you finished?" Vida suddenly became aware the waitress and Colton were looking at her.

"Yes, thank you." Vida turned to the waitress and

asked, "Could I get a to-go box?" Both Colton and the waitress looked at her almost empty plate.

"Be right back." The waitress left to go get the box. Colton didn't say anything to her when the waitress returned, silently watching as she put the remains of her meal in the box then waited expectantly for her to finish the coffee.

"Ready?" Colton rose to his feet, going to the cash register to pay. Vida waited patiently by the door, watching as the waitress flirted with him now that Vida's presence wasn't stymieing her.

The two men sitting at a nearby table smiled at her, Vida turned her eyes away, not wanting to encourage their attention. It didn't matter, within seconds the younger of the two got up from the table, finally brave enough to approach her.

"Me and my friend think we recognize you from the Purple Pussycat. Aren't you Trouble?"

"Yes, she is, so you better move along before it finds you," Colton said from behind the young man, who jumped when he heard the threatening voice behind him.

"Sorry, man, just curious."

"Yeah, well curiosity got the cat killed." The man practically ran back to his seat at Colton's threat.

"That happen a lot?" Colton asked, glaring at the embarrassed man's friend smirking from the table.

"Some," Vida responded evasively.

"At school?" he probed.

"No, thank God." Colton held the door open for her and Vida walked through the doorway, aware of several sets of eyes watching their departure.

She climbed on Colton's bike after putting the helmet back on. He never wore a helmet, but he refused to let her ride without one. The restaurant was only a block away from the apartment; Vida wished it was a longer ride. She had grown to enjoy riding with Colton; he was a good driver and handled the bike expertly.

Colton unlocked his apartment door, letting her go through first. Vida came to a dead stop seeing Tessa sprawled across the couch completely naked. Vida tried not to let her mouth hang open, but didn't think she was successful. She didn't know why it shocked her so much. After working at the strip club, nudity should have become familiar to her, yet she thought it was simply the surprise of finding Tessa with all her assets on display right on the very couch where she usually slept.

"What the fuck?" Vida felt Colton come to a stop behind her.

Tessa's face was priceless. Vida didn't think the woman appreciated that she was standing and gawking at her. The woman's face turned a dark red as she jumped up from the couch, pulling on her clothes.

"What the hell is she doing here?" she screamed at Colton.

"Don't worry why she's here. You need to get out, now." Colton came further into the room and closed the door behind him. Vida jumped at the sound of the slamming door.

"I need to take a shower," Vida said, moving towards the bathroom.

"You need to get out. Colton and I need to talk." Tessa tried to regain control now that her clothes were back on her body.

"You have something to talk to me about, talk to me tomorrow at the shop," Colton told the woman. Vida almost felt sorry for Tessa. Pulling her gown and robe out of the hall closet, she tried to ignore their voices as she went into the bathroom. The loud yells were smothered with the water as she turned on the shower.

Vida took her time showering, washing her hair, shaving her legs and then combing and braiding her hair. Dreading going back into the living room, she was relieved to find it empty. Putting her to-go box in the refrigerator, she carried her sheets and blankets to the couch. Pausing, she hurriedly flipped over the cushions then laid out the sheet on the couch and neatly made it up for the night.

The front door opened just as she finished with the couch and Vida saw him hesitate after it had closed. When his eyes then brushed over her body in the blue toweling robe and neatly braided hair, Vida's stomach clenched at the look in his eyes.

"I'm sorry about that. I didn't know she had a key. That won't happen again." Vida would take that bet. Tessa had been humiliated in front of Vida. No woman would risk that twice in a lifetime.

"It's all right. I'm sure she was as embarrassed as I was," Vida lied.

"That's doubtful." Vida saw the anger in his face, glad that it wasn't directed towards her.

Running his hand through his hair, his frustrated sigh filled the silent room. "I'm going to bed. Need anything?" He paused before leaving, waiting for her reply.

"No thanks." He gave a sharp nod at her reply.

Vida turned out the lights before lying down. She had actually slept better the last two weeks in his apartment than she had in a long time. Colton's presence made her feel safer than she had felt in King's guarded nightclub. Vida's mind shied away from figuring out why, snuggling down into the warm blanket and letting the sound of the shower lull her to sleep.

Chapter Six

Vida woke with a start when Colton shook her shoulder.

"Shake that ass; we're running late." Vida sat up; looking out the window to see the sun was bright. Forgetting that she was only in her t-shirt, Vida jumped from the couch then, disoriented, she tripped over her backpack and fell against Colton before he could move out of her way. Putting her hands on his chest to regain her balance, Colton's hands landed on her hips to steady her.

"You all right?" His voice sounded amused.

Vida nodded. "Sorry," she mumbled, moving away towards the hall. She picked out clean clothes, went into the bathroom, and pulled on loose jeans and an oversized shirt. She hurriedly brushed out her hair before pulling it back.

She was in the kitchen eating her leftovers from Waffle House when Colton came into the kitchen. Giving her a sour look, he pulled out a box of cereal and made himself a bowl before joining her at the table.

Vida finished eating, licked off the last of the syrup from her lip and was rising from the table with her plate when Colton's eyes caught hers. Vida froze, she had seen that look enough on the men's faces in the front row to know exactly what it meant. Quickly averting her gaze, Vida washed her plate before putting it in the drainer to dry.

Gathering what she would need for the day, she put her recharged computer into her backpack while waiting for Colton to wash his bowl. Getting his keys, they went outside to the motorcycle. Vida ignored the tension-filled silence from Colton, grabbing his waist when he throttled the engine.

She had promises to keep and future plans that a man like Colton would derail. He obviously enjoyed a variety of women and Vida had no intentions of being just another piece of gum he chewed and discarded.

Sawyer, Vida and Callie had made promises to each other that they wouldn't grow up to be like their mothers. Vida's own mother would fall in love with any man who wanted her, making her false promises that were never kept. Each time Vida watched her mother sink further and further into depression, blaming herself because it never worked out.

Sawyer's father had been killed in a car accident, devastating her mother. She had never sought solace in another's arms. She had held her heart untouched by another until the day a vicious mugger had taken her life for twenty dollars in ones and some change.

Callie's mother had been by far the worst. Even now, Vida's mind shied away from thinking about the monster that had given birth to such a beautiful child, both in body and spirit. She had used men to her own advantage and had been a ruthless, money-grabbing whore.

Vida felt tears and had to swallow the lump in her throat at the thought of Callie and the promises the three had made each other. Their bubble gum promises had seemed so simple in their childhood, yet they remained unfulfilled. Sawyer was held at the mercy of an unknown man, Vida found herself in the same job that her mother had been unable to escape and Callie hadn't even made it out of childhood alive; a victim of the very life that had created her. The wind dried the tears that Vida couldn't prevent from falling.

Colton drove the bike to the side of the tattoo shop where Vida climbed off as soon as he stopped and then, without waiting for him, she rushed into the shop. The lobby was empty, but Tessa, hearing the bell, came into the room. Her expression showed she wasn't any happier than she had been the night before.

Ignoring Vida, she turned her anger towards Colton. "You were supposed to be here an hour ago. I rescheduled your client for twelve. Since you're so late, you can make the time up during your lunch hour." Vida didn't think Colton was going to be happy with Tessa's bossy attitude.

Vida tried to ignore the tense situation as she sat behind the desk. She pulled out her computer and turned it on.

"Let's not forget who the boss is here, Tessa. I called from the apartment and had already rescheduled the appointment. Call him back and ask which time he prefers."

Tessa stiffened. "I ran this shop while you were in prison; it's more mine than yours."

"Don't forget who is the one responsible for putting me in prison, Tessa. I bought this shop with my own money. Now that I'm out, I've told you that you need to move on. There are other shops in town who would be happy to give you a job." His deadly calm voice had Vida glancing up from her computer. She had no doubt that Colton could be a mean son of a bitch.

"I'm not leaving!" she yelled.

Colton shrugged. "Then don't, but you're not going to boss me around and bitch at me every five seconds. If you stay, you're just another employee to me."

"Colton, I'm your wife."

"Actually, in thirty days you will be my ex-wife," Colton informed her.

"You filed the papers?" Vida could see the shock on Tessa's face.

"I signed the papers the day after I was released from prison. I told you to take care of it, you didn't. I did." Unremorsefully, he continued, "Now all we have left is a business relationship, one I no longer want, but I will leave that to you. Me and you, in any other way, does not exist. Do you fucking understand me, Tessa?"

Tessa's pale face stared back at Colton mutely before storming from the room.

"I think you should tell her why I'm staying with you. It will calm her down," Vida advised. "I really don't want her blaming me for you wanting a divorce."

"Tessa knows exactly who is responsible for our divorce," Colton said grimly.

"Then why is she throwing all these dirty looks at me?" Vida asked in confusion.

"Because she thinks she owns me and doesn't want to admit our divorce is her fault." Colton crossed his arms over his chest, his t-shirt stretched, leaving the tats on his forearm visible. Vida's eyes traced the lines of the various tats.

"And," he continued, "she thinks I'm fucking you."

"Her name is on several of your tats; a woman begins to think a man *is* hers when he brands himself with her name. I would appreciate it if you would tell her I'm not sleeping with you. It will definitely make my day go easier when I have to deal with her clients." Vida was getting tired of Tessa's snide remarks.

"It won't matter; she won't believe me."

"Why?" Vida asked, looking down at her computer and refusing to gaze into his eyes.

"Because Tessa knows that I like to fuck. She won't believe there is the slightest chance that you could live with me and not have me put my cock in your tight little pussy." Colton's voice became intimately suggestive.

Shocked, Vida looked up into his face. For the last two weeks he had completely ignored her presence, treating her with cold indifference, now he was talking to her in a way that was sexually explicit. Something didn't add up and Vida was pretty sure she knew the answer to Colton's big change.

"King wouldn't let you get rid of me, would he?" Mischievous laughter erupted as Vida was unable to hold back. She could practically see the smoke coming out of his ears. Desperately trying to dampen down her amusement before he strangled her, Vida gathered her control. It wasn't easy, but she finally succeeded.

"You think you have it all figured out, don't you?" Colton questioned, neither confirming nor denying his plan.

"Damn, Colton, I think I'm smart enough to know that the last thing you want is me in your apartment. If King refused to let me leave, your only other option is to get me to want to leave," she mocked him, leaning back in the swivel chair and placing her arms across her chest.

"What you didn't think about is that I actually don't mind living with you, despite your revolving bedroom door. It's better than sleeping in the same room as one of King's women, who are giving blowjobs or fucking before I can get out of the room. It's damn sure better than letting Digger get me and it sure as hell is better than leaving before I find Sawyer." Vida's voice was practically yelling at Colton as he stood dumbfounded at the woman he had mistaken for being a timid little mouse.

Vida almost started laughing again at his expression, but decided she had pressed her luck far enough for the day. The bell rang, letting them know a customer was coming in the door. Seth came towards the counter with a genuine smile on his face, carrying his computer.

"I'm off today. I thought if it's okay with you that I would hang around and. when you weren't busy, you could help me code?" Seth nervously waited for her reply.

Vida returned his smile with one of her own. "I'd enjoy it, Seth. I get bored between customers now that most of my classes are finished."

Colton just stared back and forth between the two for several seconds.

"Make sure you keep track of the clients," was all he said before disappearing.

The day was much better with Seth keeping her company. Tessa merely eyed Seth when she came out front. Vida could tell she was wondering just what their relationship was, but she didn't ask and Vida wasn't about to volunteer the information.

Colton came out with his client; a woman, not much older than Vida, who had wanted a tat of an owl on her shoulder. She had gushed her admiration of his tats when she had caught sight of him. It wasn't much better now that her tattoo had been completed and wrapped.

Colton had been about to call his next appointment when the woman grabbed his arm, keeping him by her side. "Call me?" Vida had become used to the forwardness of the women that came into Colton's shop.

"Sure thing, sugar." Colton gave her a smile that looked insincere to Vida, but she was also sure that she would see the bleached blond doing the walk out of Colton's front door during the wee hours when he was done with her.

"Colton, my man, I see you still have the touch."

Everyone's eyes turned towards the loud voice to see a middle-aged man standing in the doorway, letting the door close behind him as he came further into the room. He was extremely attractive with hard angles, yet laugh lines were leading away from his amused eyes as they took in the young girl pleading for Colton's attention.

"I see three years in the state pen hasn't hurt your mojo any." The man was as large as his voice.

"Shut-up, Max," Colton said, trying to disentangle himself from the grip, which had tightened on his arm.

"You've been in prison?" Instead of fear, Vida clearly saw arousal on the woman's face.

"Yeah, I just got out a couple of weeks ago," Colton answered.

"You sure you don't want me to wait around until you get off? I don't mind waiting." She moved closer to Colton.

"I'm sure, Lara. I'm busy tonight. I'll call you next week." Vida rolled her eyes, more like he had another woman scheduled for tonight.

Lara paid her bill then left when it became obvious that Colton wouldn't change his mind. Vida sat beside Seth, reaching out to point to a figure he had missed, feeling the eyes of the newcomer on her. She steadily ignored the curious eyes on her as she heard him talking to Colton.

"Have I met you? Your face seems familiar to me for some reason." The silence in the room forced Vida to look up, knowing the voice was addressing her.

"I don't think so, I would have remembered." It was the honest truth; the man was very striking, both in features and in the way he dressed. By his looks and from the motorcycle he owned that was parked outside the glass door, Vida assumed he was in a motorcycle club. He had on jeans and a t-shirt with a leather jacket that had several patches on it, most held a club name that was constantly in the news for the criminal activities it was said they had committed.

"I think we have. You seem too familiar..." Vida knew the instant he recognized her, amusement and admiration lit his face.

"Trouble?" He laughed and hit his hand against Colton's back. "I have died and gone to Heaven." Holding his arms out, he gave her a devilish grin. "Come to daddy."

Blood rushed up her from her chest to land with bright flags of shame on her cheeks as Seth stopped coding to stare at her as if he had never seen her before. His mouth dropped open.

"You work in King's club?" Before Vida could reply, Max barged into their conversation.

"She sure does. You have the pleasure of sitting next to one of King's gloriously divine exotic dancers, Trouble."

Seth looked at her with horrified eyes, as if the computer he had in front of him was about to be stolen. Vida's emotions closed down. It was a look she was very familiar with, she had seen it dozens of times when she was a child, whenever someone found out her mother was a stripper.

Seth closed his computer, gathered his papers and shoved them unceremoniously into his backpack.

"I better be going. I'll talk to you later, Vida." Seth jumped from his chair, taking off from the shop as if the hounds of hell were after him. Vida swallowed down the hurt; she had thought they were friends. Seth hadn't made any sexual overtures towards her and it had made her relax in his easygoing company.

"I take it the kid didn't know." Vida could see remorse in Max's eyes.

Vida shrugged, refusing to let them see she was hurting. "It was my fault; I had plenty of time to tell him."

"Who gives a fuck, if something like that runs off the little pussy. You're better off without him," Max stated.

Vida shrugged again, Seth had surprised her by his abrupt departure. It wasn't Max's fault he had inadvertently let it out that she was stripping, it was her own for entangling herself in the mess her life had become. Not for the first time, Vida questioned whether she was doing the right thing, wishing she had other options where Sawyer was concerned. Maybe she should go to the police again?

Vida ran her hand along the computer, feeling the cold metal against her fingertips. She gathered back her control.

King was her only hope of getting Sawyer back; she knew that in her heart. She had taken the only road open to her, so now she had to tough out the repercussions.

When Sawyer was back, she could leave and move somewhere where people had never heard of her mother and wouldn't have to be constantly on guard about being recognized as a stripper. She just had to hang on to her tattered pride until then.

Pasting a fake smile on her lips that she was unaware didn't reach her eyes, she forestalled any other comments. "You're right. I was only doing him a favor anyway, helping him with his video game. Are you wanting to get a tattoo?" she asked Max, trying to change the subject.

"Only if Colton has an opening. I don't want that bitch of a wife anywhere near me with those needles of hers." Max shuddered, giving her a wink.

"Colton's free; you can go on back with him." Vida smiled at the man's antics.

"Thanks, I am sorry, sometimes my mouth spouts out shit before I think." Max moved closer to the counter.

"It's really okay." This time Vida's smile was much warmer. "But I'm still not going to give you a private dance," she teased. She could tell he was upset with himself for being responsible for Seth leaving.

His heartbreak lasted three seconds. "I guess I'll survive. Any chance you'll give me the redhead's number that comes on the stage after you?"

Vida studied Colton's friend, he seemed like a really nice guy. "I'll give her a call. If she says it cool, I'll give it to you. I will warn you, though, she does have a boyfriend."

"Trouble, you just made my day. I'll make sure we name our firstborn after you." Vida couldn't hold back her laughter at his silly response.

"I'll hold you to that," she mock threatened.

"Go on back to my room, I'll be there in a minute," Colton told Max, staring intently at Vida.

Colton waited until Max had left the room before questioning Vida.

"You sure you're okay?" His eyes searched hers.

"I'm fine. It was only a matter of time before Seth found out. The semester is almost over and when Sawyer comes home, I'll be leaving. So it's really not a big deal."

"Leaving? Where will you be going?" His sharp voice surprised Vida. Just minutes ago he had been trying to get rid of her.

"I want to travel. Just get in a car and drive until I come to a place I want to stay," Vida answered.

"It's not safe for a woman to travel by herself." Vida stared at the big, bad, tatted man staring down at her. Wherever she went was safer than Queen City, Texas.

"I won't be by myself, Sawyer will be with me," Vida countered his argument.

"I hope everything works out, Vida, I really do," Colton said doubtfully.

Vida replied with resolve in her voice. "It will."

Colton turned, but Vida saw the pity in his expression. She knew he thought that King wouldn't get Sawyer back, however Vida had put all her faith in him. He had promised Vida when her mother died that if she ever needed anything, she only had to ask. She never expected to need King, but with Sawyer's disappearance, she had no choice. He had agreed to help her, and Vida knew it was because of her mother, yet a look had momentarily crossed his ruthless face when she had told him of Sawyer's disappearance.

It had been fear.

* * *

They grabbed a bite to eat on the way home, neither saying much. Vida wanted to maintain a distance between her and Colton; a distance she felt slipping away. Colton seemed to feel the same way, with his familiar cold expression in place; he didn't attempt any conversation to fill the uneasy silence between them.

When they arrived back at the apartment, Vida went into the bathroom to get ready for that night's performance. She shaved her legs, made sure her bikini area was cleanly shaven and then rubbed an erotic smelling cream onto her skin, giving her skin a golden sheen.

She curled and fluffed her hair, making sure she used extra hairspray so that the bike helmet didn't do too much damage. Dressing in sweatpants and her college jersey, she put her make-up and brushes into her backpack. Finally finished, she went back out into the apartment to find that Colton was still in his room.

A knock on the door had her going toward it, looking through the peephole she saw Henry. She opened the door and stepped back to let him inside the apartment.

"You ready?" he asked.

"You're taking me tonight?" Vida asked, surprised. Colton hadn't mentioned that he wasn't taking her as he usually did after they ate dinner.

"Colton called King and asked if I could give you a ride tonight," Henry replied.

"Oh." Vida tried not to feel hurt, but did, not knowing why. "I'm ready. Let me grab my bag."

Henry waited patiently by the door as Vida picked up her backpack from the table. Unable to stop herself, her eyes slid to the closed bedroom door. Turning back to Henry, she closed and locked the door behind them. The ride in the back of King's car seemed confining after becoming used to traveling on the back of Colton's bike.

Henry opened the door for her when they arrived. "You're quiet tonight, Vida. Anything wrong?"

Vida shook her head. "Nothing, just wish this was all over." Henry looked back at her in sympathy, although he didn't say anything as he escorted her inside. His loyalty to King was without question. In the dressing room, Vida changed into her black, sheer outfit, her tiny black bra exposed under the sheer material. She liked this three piece set better than the red. The three piece set gave her less time to spend naked.

When she was ready, she went to the curtain to wait her queue. As the music began, Vida swallowed hard and stepped forward.

Chapter Seven

Vida unlocked the apartment door, turning to wave back at Henry that everything was okay before going inside. Flipping on the light switch, she turned and locked the door. Dropping her backpack onto the chair, she went into the small kitchen to get a cold bottle of water before she took a quick shower to wash away the filth from the club she still felt clinging to her.

She refilled the bottle with water from the sink and was putting it back into the refrigerator to get cold when she heard the bedroom door open and footsteps coming down the hallway. Vida kept her face expressionless as the waitress from the Waffle House came into the room looking disheveled and stinking from sex. Colton walking behind her paused as they both became aware that they were no longer alone. The waitress, now in jeans and a pink top, was obviously on her way out. Colton, wearing only jeans that he had zipped but hadn't buttoned, was shirtless, exposing his chest covered in a variety of tattoos.

"I didn't know you lived with her." The waitress looked accusingly at Colton.

"He doesn't, I'm just a temporary roommate," Vida

explained quickly. The woman looked like she was about to throw a hissy fit. She was all about letting Colton handle it, but Vida was tired and didn't want to listen to yet another woman take another sarcastic remark from Colton, which she could tell from the steely look on his face he was about to give her.

"Oh, then I guess that's all right." Suspiciously she glared at Vida, who decided the best thing to do was to ignore them both. Getting her nightclothes, she went into the bathroom, unable to hear the words exchanged between the two of them.

Vida wished just one time she could have an uneventful night without any of Colton's fuck buddies coming and going. She was beginning to think the room at King's wasn't all that bad.

Coming out of the bathroom after she was dressed in her flannel pajamas and her hair brushed backed into a tight braid, she saw Colton leaning against the counter in the kitchen.

Ignoring him, she plucked her sheets and blankets from the closet and started making up the couch.

"I didn't need you to butt in and explain anything to Tammy. It was none of her business."

Vida shrugged. "Sorry, next time I'll keep my mouth shut." Finished, she laid down on the couch and pulled the blanket over her. "Could you turn off the light?"

Colton stood tautly for several seconds before walking to the light switch and turning it off.

Vida heard his footsteps leave the room and then turned on her side to make herself more comfortable. Trampling down the unexpected jealousy, it took several minutes to calm her nerves before she relaxed enough to fall asleep.

Vida woke the next morning, determined to finish the last of her course assignments. She set her computer up at the table and began her work only to stop long enough to fix herself a cup of coffee. She was so engrossed in her work, she wasn't aware of Colton coming into the room. It was only when he sat down at the table across from her that she was drawn away from studying her book.

"When do your classes end?"

"This week," Vida answered his question, watching as he took a drink of his coffee.

"After your class is over, I want you to leave town, find someplace to hole up. I'll help King find Sawyer and bring her to you when I can."

"Why would you become involved?"

"I'm already involved. It's only a matter of time before Digger finds out you're staying here. It will actually be easier for both of us if you leave town. It will draw Digger's attention away from you."

Disappointment filled Vida; she hadn't thought that Colton would be worried about Digger coming after him. He was right, Digger knew everything going on in town, and he probably already knew that she was no longer staying at the club.

"You're right, I didn't think about your safety. We don't have to wait until my class is over, I can—"

Colton set his cup down hard, spilling the remaining coffee over the side. "I'm not worried about Digger coming after me, but if he's as smart as I know he is, the son of a bitch will know your classes are almost over. If you went missing, it would make all the papers, the headlines alone of a young college girl's disappearance is the only thing holding him back. Once your classes are over, he can make you disappear and everyone will just think that you moved on. Exactly what you said you were going to do last night."

Vida's mouth snapped closed. What he was saying was the truth. She had even told a couple of her friends at school her plans.

"I can't leave without Sawyer. We made a promise when we were kids that we would both leave town together. I can't break my promise."

"Dammit." Colton brushed his hand through his already tumbled hair. "This is a fucked up mess."

Vida silently agreed with him.

Standing up from the table, he wiped the spilt coffee from the table. "Get dressed; we're going out."

"Where to?"

"I don't know, but I'm sick of being cooped up. I need some fresh air and, since I can't leave you alone, that means you're coming with me."

Vida started to protest, but she hadn't had a free day in so long she had forgotten what it was like simply to go out and have fun. Closing down her computer, she went into the bathroom and changed into jeans and a long sleeved shirt. Colton had dressed and was sitting on the chair in the living room waiting for her.

"Ready?"

"Yes."

It was early afternoon, so not many people were out on the roads. He drove them out of the city where the light traffic dwindled down until they only passed a car every so often. The scenery lulled Vida into forgetting her problems; the drawback was it increased her awareness of Colton. Sitting against his back with her thighs so close had her wanting things her mind refused to acknowledge. Her body on the other hand had a mind of its own.

He handled the bike expertly, making Vida wonder how he had learned to ride the bike so well in the city.

Eventually, they rode through a small town where Colton stopped for gas. It was next door to a restaurant where they went through the drive- thru. Vida sat on the bike as Colton stood next to it, eating their food. When they finished, Colton drove down a small, paved road on a large piece of land. They found a farmers' market, which had been set up on the side of the road.

"Let's check it out," Colton said suddenly.

Vida agreed and they spent an amusing couple of hours going to the various booths. Vida bought some fruit while

Colton purchased drinks and a couple of sandwiches. Finding a spot on the ground away from the booths, they ate quietly as they watched the customers shop.

"I love being out of the city," Vida said, looking at the countryside surrounding them.

Colton paused at eating his sandwich. It was the first thing Vida had shared about herself. The woman kept herself so contained, you never knew what she was thinking.

"You don't like the city?"

"I hate it. I like being out in open spaces. The idea of having just a few neighbors and having a small town sense of community where they actually care about one another appeals to me."

"But you have that in the city. Your relationship with Sawyer proves that," Colton argued.

Vida shook her head. "Sawyer, Callie and I all lived on the fifth floor in a low income housing building. Sawyer's mother would babysit Callie and me while my mom worked or Callie's was busy. But none of them shared anything about their lives. The apartment building was filled with people who weren't even supposed to be living there. Everyone minded their own business because they didn't want anyone sticking their nose into theirs or the possibility of getting evicted."

There was definitely no sense of community where she had grown up. Vida watched the people at the farmers' market greet each other, standing and talking amongst themselves before continuing with their shopping.

"I see your point." Colton recognized that she wanted a tight community to replace her lack of family until she had one of her own. Colton didn't know why that thought bothered him, only that it did.

Her dark hair was pulled back, showing her high cheekbones and green eyes. Her red lips bit into a piece of melon that had juice running down her chin. Giving her a napkin, he watched as she wiped away the juice from her face and licked her lips to catch the stray droplets. Her unconscious sensuality hardened his cock. Colton shifted on the hard ground.

Taking an apple for himself, he watched her pick up another piece of melon and had to force his attention back to what she was saying.

"In a town like this, a child like Callie would never have suffered. A neighbor, school or friend would have reported her mother. She might still be alive if she hadn't had the misfortune to live where she did."

"You don't know that, Vida. Maybe she would still be alive or maybe something else could have killed her. She might have died some other way and never known what it was like to have such wonderful friends as you or Sawyer."

"She was so special, Colton. Her mother would drop her off as often as Sawyer's mother would take her during the day. All three of us didn't realize we weren't sisters until we were about five-years-old; we spent so much time together. Especially Sawyer and me because our mothers were friends and they would swap out babysitting. Brenda, that bitch, would only let Sawyer's mom babysit when she was coming off her high. She wanted Callie by her side all the time, even when she was..." Her voice broke off.

"My mom and Sawyer's mom both reported her to social services when the bruises became worse, but they always gave her back to that bitch, then she started threatening our moms. She held a knife to my mom one night when she tried to talk to her. She even threatened Sawyer and me if they didn't mind their own business."

"Vida," Colton tried to stop her, knowing where this story ended, seeing no need for her to take this trip down memory lane. Goldie had told him about Callie's mother. He had wanted to have a talk with her himself, but Goldie had been terrified that the woman would disappear with Callie.

She continued on, lost in her own story, "The first time Sawyer and I saw Marshall, he scared us; he was so frightening." Vida could still see the white haired, muscular man who had been as large as a giant to the small children they were then.

"He scared me, too, and I wasn't a little girl." Colton tried again to regain her attention unsuccessfully.

"The sad part is, I think he really cared for Callie; she gained weight and didn't have as many bruises. Sawyer and I were happy that he'd moved in with her mom. Do you think he meant to hurt Callie when he killed Brenda?" Vida buried her face in her hands. "I still see her face every day, Colton, wishing I had smelled the smoke sooner, got to her door faster, knocked louder. There should have been something I could have done."

"I heard about that fire, Vida. It was in all the papers and it was all anyone could talk about for weeks in the neighborhood. There was nothing you could have done. When Marshall caught Brenda in bed with another man, he went crazy and killed them both. Callie must have managed to escape out of the window because they found her body hiding in one of the vacant apartments. She was probably so scared from what she'd witnessed that she had run and hid, and was too frightened to come out when she heard the sirens."

"She was only eight-years-old."

"Sweetheart, you were only a year older. You did exactly what you were supposed to do. You tried to alert them then got outside with your mom. That was why you lived," Colton tried to reason with her.

Vida came back to the present with her hand in Colton's. Self-consciously, she pulled it away and began cleaning up the remains of their impromptu picnic.

They passed back through the booths as they left and a young girl with a woman standing by a cardboard box drew Vida's attention. She paused and looked into the box where a reddish-blond ball of fluff stared back at her.

"Awe, isn't it cute." Vida bent down and petted the squirming puppy that promptly started smothering her in puppy kisses. Giggling, Vida stroked the curly soft fur. "Is it a girl or boy?"

"It's a girl," the little girl replied. "It's the last one I have left. Mama wouldn't let me name her cause we have to sell them, but I think she looks like a Chloe."

The little girl cast her mother a sidelong look. Shaking her head at the little girl with a soft smile, the mother reached into the box and handed her the wiggling puppy. Burying her face in the soft puppy fur, this was what Vida wanted out of life, normalcy. It sounded boring, but Vida could easily see the love and happiness shining from the mother and child.

"I'm selling her for two hundred fifty dollars. She's a malti-poo." Vida stroked the soft fur one more time before regretfully giving it back.

"I wish I could buy her, but right now I don't have a permanent home. It's going to be a while before I can have a puppy." Reluctantly, Vida gave the puppy back to the little girl, who took it back with a relieved smile.

"I wish you could have taken her. I can tell you two would have made a great match." The woman smiled. Vida glanced down at the little girl who didn't try to hide her joy at having her puppy back.

Vida said goodbye with a last look at the wiggling puppy in the little girl's arms. Her stomach clenched as she tried to gather her emotions around her while they walked back to the bike. Colton stiffened as they drew closer, not understanding why until she saw two men touching his bike. One kicked the wheel while another messed with the handlebar.

"Get away from my ride," Colton said as he moved toward the men.

"We're just lookin' at it." The man had tobacco in his mouth, spitting a stream of juice near Colton's foot. Vida assumed the man was an idiot until her gaze went to the side and saw another large man leaning against the side of an older model truck.

"Go find something else to look at, like your wife fucking your brother."

The man cockily pulled up his saggy pants and raised his hands in the air.

"I don't want no trouble. What make is it? You get plenty of pussy ridin' on those nut busters? Been thinking of getting me one. If it gets me a piece of pussy that looks like her, I might need to buy one."

"Shithead, you couldn't afford what a bike like that costs, but you go ahead and buy one you can afford because a dumb fuck like you would be road kill in a hour."

The man turned red. Vida thought he might have swallowed the wad of tobacco in his mouth, instead he let go of another spew of juice and this time it landed on Colton's boot.

Vida was watching it and still didn't see it happen. One minute the man was standing there and the next his face was planted in Colton's boot with Colton's hand in his hair. He was using the man's face to wipe the offensive stuff off his boot.

"What the fuck." His friends rushed forward.

Colton used his other foot to kick the downed man away from him. The first man to reach him had a fist shoved in his nose and blood flew as he was knocked back into his other friend that was also coming at Colton, causing them both to lose their balance. Before they could right themselves, Colton beat the men mercilessly.

Vida stood there, open mouthed, as people from the farmers' market tried to break the fight apart.

"You need to get the hell out of here," the friendly mother told Vida and Colton. "Those boys have several friends in town. They won't like it that one man beat up all three of them."

"We're going." Colton waited until Vida was on the bike before he got on and started the motor.

Colton drove them back to the city, and as each mile

brought them closer, Vida felt the return of all her worries that she had been able to briefly put from her mind.

As soon as they were back in the apartment, Vida took a quick shower before going back to her homework. The life that mother and daughter shared was the future she was working so hard toward. She had to keep her mind on that, not the reaction Colton aroused in her. He was nothing more than a one-way ticket to reliving her mother's life.

* * *

Colton had watched Vida shut down her emotions when she walked away from the small girl and puppy. She had wanted that small dog so much it was almost tangible. Colton had begun to notice during the short time Vida had been around him that the more strongly she felt about something, the more she shut down her emotions.

He couldn't understand it. Goldie had been a good mother, she had constantly talked about Vida when they had been at the same party or hung out with mutual friends. He was sure that she hadn't secretly abused Vida, so he couldn't understand why she was so closed within herself. The only thing he could think of was that with her mom dead and Sawyer gone, she was overwhelmed and closing down was her way of dealing with the situation she had found herself in.

He had to respect the way she handled herself. Vida was determined to make a successful life for herself, wanting her friend by her side when she accomplished her goals.

Colton remembered seeing Sawyer before he went to prison. She had come into his shop for a small tattoo on the inside of her wrist. She was tall and curvy. He could easily see why she had been kidnapped with her fresh-faced beauty. Others of a more corrupt nature would seek to destroy that beauty and innocence that was easily discernable, even if all she was wearing were cheap jeans and a t-shirt.

He didn't know why, but for some reason, her tattoo came to mind. He had given hundreds and actually remembered only the ones he had created or he had done extremely well in spite of their difficulty. Sawyer's had been simple and straightforward. She had only wanted a simple word on her wrist. Freedom.

Colton was beginning to think that the three young girls he remembered playing outside when they were little had been imprisoned much longer than he was.

Deciding to take a shower, he left Vida doing whatever it was she did on her computer. Washing his body then his hair, he thought about getting it cut, he always wore it long, but now it was brushing his shoulders, and he was becoming aggravated when he forgot to tie it back.

He leaned his head against the shower wall. His cock was driving him insane after feeling her lush body against his back all day. He had known it would be a mistake to spend the day with Vida, but hadn't been able to resist the temptation to get to know her better.

Colton got out of the shower, drying himself off and wrapping a towel around his hips before going into his bedroom. Forcing himself not to check out what Vida was doing, he shut the bedroom door behind him.

Picking up the cell phone on the table beside his bed, he made a call that he hoped would keep him out of trouble.

* * *

Vida heard the knock on the door and was rising from the table to answer the door when Colton's bedroom door opened and he came out dressed only in jeans. Sitting back down, Vida lowered her eyes back to the computer, already knowing it was a woman at the door; it just remained to be seen which woman he'd called.

Vida recognized the voice of the woman that he had given a tat to last week.

"What's she doing here? I thought it was just going to be the two of us. I'm really not interested in a threesome."

Vida would have laughed if she weren't so miserable.

"It's just us. Vida is just my temporary roommate. Let's go back to my bedroom."

Vida couldn't resist looking up for a second to see Colton take Lara's hand and lead her down the hallway to his bedroom. She turned away before they could catch her staring. Vida continued working for another hour, having to turn up the volume on her headphones to drone out the female screams and moans coming from the bedroom.

From past experience, Vida shut down her computer and made her bed, determined to be asleep before the woman left. Inexplicably, she didn't want to see her after she had been in Colton's bed.

Leaving on her headphones this time, Vida didn't put the pillow over her face. She lay quietly, listening to her music, pretending she was far away in a new home with Sawyer as her roommate.

For once, her plans of the future didn't comfort her.

Chapter Eight

Vida had just finished scheduling an appointment when her cell phone rang.

"Hello?" she answered hesitantly, not familiar with the number on display.

"Vida?" a woman's voice she recognized answered.

"Jazz?"

"Yes, Vida I need a big favor. Cody fell off his bike and broke his arm. We're in the emergency room. Vida, I can't leave him." Vida felt bad for the young mother who worked as a body shot girl to keep a roof over her two young children's head. They had a deadbeat dad who refused to pay his child support, but Jazz wasn't deterred her from going to school part-time during the day to get her kids a better life.

"What do you need?" Vida asked.

"I'm scheduled to work a party. It's a divorce celebration." Vida could hear the hiccup in her voice where she had been crying. "If I miss it, King will fire me. I had to miss so much work lately with the kids. He warned me if I cancelled again, he would let me go. I can't lose this job." Another hiccupping sob and Vida caved.

"What time is it?"

"In an hour. You don't have to worry about a costume I have an extra one; it's in my locker. Juliet is working it too, so you won't have to do it alone."

"I'll cover you. Don't worry, Jazz. Just take care of Cody."

"Thanks, Vida." The worried mother hung up the phone.

"Ready?" Colton asked as he came into the lobby with his keys in his hand.

"Yes. Can you give me a ride to Kings?"

"You're not scheduled for tonight." Colton stated angered that King was making her work an extra night.

"I'm not, but a friend's child got hurt and I told her I would work the party for her," Vida explained.

"Have you worked a party before?" Colton asked sharply.

"No, but if I don't, King will fire Jazz, and she has two kids, Colton."

Colton lips tightened as she grabbed her backpack. Closing and locking the doors, he let his silence speak as to what he thought about her working the party. The silence continued even after he dropped her off at the back door. Assuming he would go on to the apartment, she didn't watch as he drove around the side of the building.

Hurriedly, with not much time left, Vida went to Jazz's locker, taking a step back when she saw the outfit staring at her. It was a thong with a little black skirt that every time she moved would sway to show her ass. The top was a sheer black lace bikini top that tied closed between the breasts. Anyone barely tugging the string would expose her breasts.

"Hurry up, Vida." Juliet came into the dressing room, already dressed. Applying her make-up, she gave Vida a cold glare. "I'm not working those horny bastards myself. I already told Jazz when she called you that you better pull your weight."

Crap. Vida disliked Juliet out of all the staff King had. She used her body and wiles doing anything and everything to score the big tips.

Taking the costume from the locker, Vida went into the restroom to get dressed, not wanting to get changed under Juliet's scrutiny. Looking in the mirror when she was dressed in the costume, Vida almost changed her mind. Stiffening her shoulders and remembering the two children depending on their mother had Vida stepping back into the dressing room to brush her hair and apply her make-up.

"Hurry up." Juliet held the door open and Vida followed her up the steps to the VIP room where the party of men were waiting.

When Juliet opened the door, the group of eight men sitting at a table on two couches at the back of the room started calling for them.

Vida and Juliet both grabbed a tray of drinks and walked to the table. Each man grabbed a cup of the foaming champagne, toasting the newly divorced man. He didn't look heartbroken to Vida as he stared at her breasts and rubbed her ass when she came near to hand him his drink.

Vida moved out of reach, but didn't say anything, following Juliet's lead. In the VIP room, the men were allowed to touch more, but they weren't allowed to touch a woman's mound or pull his penis out. Other than those rules, the men paid a higher cover charge to be given greater leeway with the women.

Juliet sat down on the couch next to several men at the end of the table. She reluctantly sat down next to the newly divorced man and his friends. For the next hour, Vida sat listening as he complained about his ex-wife while she refilled their drinks.

It was after their third round of drinks that Vida noticed that Colton had come into the room and was talking with the bartender. Ignoring him, she picked up her tray and went back to the table.

"I'll give you five hundred for a dick shot," Vida overheard a man tell Juliet. The woman readily agreed, placing a cup of beer between the man legs.

Juliet squatted between his legs, going down with her mouth to the cup. Vida had to give the woman credit; she acted like she was giving him a blowjob using the cup instead of his cock. Grasping the cup between her lips, she took a sip, placing it back between his legs before going back for more. It was highly suggestive. The men got excited watching the woman perform.

"I'll give you five hundred for a dick shot." The divorced man, Vida had learned was named Copper, offered with a drunken smile.

"No thanks," Vida refused. Juliet threw her a disgusted look. The men went back to drinking and Juliet gave a couple more dick shots to the customers.

Vida escaped to the restroom when Copper began tugging on the string to her top. Juliet followed her, slamming the door closed behind them.

"I told you that you needed to pull your own weight. The next time someone wants an extra, you better jump to it. If you're such a good friend of Jazz's, give her the fucking money. How much do you think she could use the money you're throwing away? She's going to be taking a big hit, losing tonight's money. We usually score at least three grand." Vida's stricken expression didn't stop her from turning on her heel and leaving Vida in stunned silence.

Vida used the restroom quickly before going back outside. The men were now playing high card. Vida had seen the game before; whoever at the table picked the highest card, the other men at the table would chip in for a lap dance, dick shot or a body shot. Winner called which one he wanted.

The men each took turns picking cards. The one who won the first round chose Juliet to take a body shot off her body.

They cleared their table and Juliet laid down on it with her hands above her head. The men had each put in a hundred. Vida could see the gleam in her eyes at earning the eight hundred dollars. Vida watched one of the men pour a drink on Juliet's stomach. Going on his knees beside the table, he licked the drink from her wherever the liquid went on her body. Juliet cringed when he used his tongue to lick away the liquid from between her breasts.

Finally, he moved away with cheers from the onlookers. The cards were drawn two more times with the pot getting bigger each time. Conner finally won, his eyes immediately went to Vida.

"Body shot." The pot was at twelve hundred. Vida saw the threat in Juliet's eyes if she refused. Standing up, she laid down on the table, raising her hands above her head. Feeling the men's eyes on her, she heard Colton's voice at the back of the crowd.

"I'll take a piece of that action." Everyone turned to face Colton.

"You're not part of this party. Get lost." Laughing, they turned back to Vida.

"Let me take a turn drawing a card, and I'll double the pot. If I lose," Colton nodded to Connor, "he can keep the money or decide to take the shot. What have you got to lose?"

Vida could see Copper was undecided, the money and Vida both a temptation.

"You got a deal." The cards where shuffled and Colton pulled a card. He looked at the card in Connor's hand, reaching out he then pulled one from the center of the deck, turning it over he exposed a King beating the high card of Copper's eight of spades.

"You fucking cheated," one of the men yelled.

"How did I cheat when I didn't touch the cards?" Colton said calmly. The men backed away from Vida, leaving a space for Colton to stand beside the table where she laid waiting.

Vida thought at first he would let her out of it, but she could see from his angry glare he was determined to teach her a lesson.

Cooper handed him the shot of liquor pouring it onto Vida's taut stomach, the liquor slid across her flesh. Goosebumps rose and Vida shivered as Colton gazed down on her sprawled on the table. He sank to his knees beside the low table. Any second Vida expected him to call it off, it was only when his tongue began grazing her flesh did she realize he wasn't going to stop.

His sensuous tongue rose feelings in Vida that she had never felt before, warmth pooled between her legs. Vida flushed in embarrassment as she tried to tear her gaze away from his, but Colton held her gaze with an iron will, daring her to turn away. His tongue lapped at the liquor at the band of her skirt that hung low on her hips, delving slightly beneath the band. Vida's fingers grasped the edge of the table at her head.

She tried to wiggle her hips away from his enticing touch.

"Lie still," Colton ordered. Vida stopped moving her stomach, clenching tighter.

He moved upward, tracing the path of the liquor, swallowing every drop as he moved between her breasts. Unable to help herself, Vida arched at the first touch of his tongue on the side of her breast.

"I told you to lie still." His eyes held hers. His tongue made sure every drop of liquid was found before he moved his tongue to the other breast where droplets glistened. His tongue delved underneath the skimpy top. Vida felt the tip lick her hardened nipple in a brief touch.

Before she could jump away, Colton stood up, lifting Vida back to her feet with his hands on her waist. She almost lost her balance on her high heeled shoes, it didn't help that her knees felt like jelly.

"Hell yeah, let's do that again," Conner yelled. The men

sat back down as Conner pulled Vida down to sit on his lap.

"Have a seat," one of the drunken party goers' offered Colton.

The cards came back out. Colton won the next hand and with a pot of a grand he chose Juliet to give him a dick shot. Vida turned her eyes away as the woman knelt between Colton's thighs and took a shot of beer from the cup held against his cock. Vida couldn't bring herself to watch the erotic woman's display as she became even bolder, grazing her teeth over Colton jean covered cock.

When she finished, the cards were drawn again. Vida became suspicious when he won for the third time in a row, but the drunken men had long sense lost what rationale they had.

Vida tensed, expecting him to take a body shot off Juliet, but he chose a lap dance from Vida instead. Colton's challenging stare and Juliet's jealous one had Vida rising from Copper's lap.

Moving to Colton, she watched as he leaned back sprawled in his chair waiting for her. Vida began dancing self-consciously in front of him, feeling stiff. His mocking gaze had her trying to listen more closely to the music, forcing her body to relax. The thought of Jazz getting another grand made her feel slighter better as her hips began to sway and she straddled Colton's thighs. Sitting down on his lap she moved her breasts seductively towards his chest before teasingly moving backwards. She did this several times before she finally allowed her breasts to press flat against his chest, rubbing them provocatively against him. Rising her hips and sinking back down, a bare inch separated her from his covered cock as she ground down on him, the music reaching its climax. Rising swiftly, she moved away, but Colton grabbed her hand, rising to his own feet.

Motioning to the bouncer Colton turned back to the party of men. As much money as they had wasted tonight,

Vida was sure this wouldn't be the last divorce party they attended.

"Party's over," Lou, another bouncer of King's, brought everyone's attention to him. "Your driver is downstairs waiting." The grumbling started, but quickly cut off by Lou as he moved the men towards the doorway.

"Go get changed. I'll bring my bike to the front," Colton said, leaving her in front of the dressing room.

Juliet came in as she was about to get changed with her cut of the night's money in an envelope. "I tipped the bartender and Lou."

"Thanks, Juliet." Juliet gave her a grudging nod before going to her locker to grab her coat, not bothering to change.

At Vida's questioning gaze, Juliet shrugged. "Connor offered to pay me for a private performance. I have to go; their waiting in the car for me." Vida watched the woman leave the room, not wanting to think about how Juliet would be spending the rest of her night.

Dressing took Vida several minutes. Grabbing the envelope of cash, she put it in her pocket before going out into the hallway. Vida noticed the light in the hallway was burned out. The darkened hallway gave her the creeps. While King had spared no expense to regularly redecorate the front of the club, the back was old and still had only one source of light, the one that was burnt out.

Carefully making her way, she was almost at the end when she felt someone come up behind her, putting a rough hand over her mouth, jerking her struggling body backwards. She felt herself lifted and carried to the back exit and knew if they got her out the door, that whoever it was would probably have a car waiting. Terror had her struggling harder. The grip on her tightened, making it hard to breathe.

"What the hell!" Vida heard Colton's voice, relief making her go limp.

Whoever was holding her turned to face Colton. The arm around her waist dropped away and Vida saw a flash of a knife in the dim hallway.

Colton moved forward quickly with King coming up behind him. His hand snapped out, striking the arm holding the knife. It dropped to the floor. Colton jerked Vida away as his fist slammed into the unidentified man behind her.

Freed Vida found herself behind Colton's back as King moved forward with the knife in his hand. Her assailant turned to run, but King reached him before he could open the door and escape. The man tried to struggle away from King, but King brought the knife down, plunging it into the man's chest. Throwing the now lifeless body down, King opened the back door, looking outside.

"I don't see anyone else. Get her out of here."

Colton took Vida's hand, leading her away from the man lying in the hallway in a pool of blood. Henri came in the hallway then, his quick glance taking in the situation. Vida was sure it wasn't the first time he had to clean up King's mess.

"Find out who it is then get rid of it," King ordered.

"Okay, boss." Henri moved past them.

Colton didn't give her time to ask questions. "Are you all right?" he questioned once they were outside.

"I think so, just a little shaken. Who do you think it was?"

"Probably one of Digger's men," King said, coming to stand beside Vida.

"What made you come back?" Vida asked Colton.

"Juliet warned me when she came outside the light was off back there. She thought she saw someone, but wasn't sure."

Vida reached into her pocket and pulled out the envelope of money. "Will you give this to Jazz for me?"

"Yes. Vida, you can't talk about what happened," King said, taking the envelope.

"I know. I'll keep my mouth shut," she promised before climbing onto Colton's bike.

Juliet might not like her, but she had saved Vida.

Vida grasped Colton around his waist, thankful that both King and him had been there to help. She felt a jolt of fear knowing that Digger wouldn't stop. Colton owed her nothing, barely knew her, and yet, he hadn't hesitated to protect her. She acknowledged to herself there was more to the sexy tattoo artist than she had thought possible. He just might be her saving grace.

Chapter Nine

Vida came out of the classroom looking for Henry, surprised when she didn't see him. Colton had dropped her off before class and Henry should have been here to pick her up. Feeling nervous at the strange occurrence, Vida stayed close to the classroom building where there were several students milling around.

Out of the corner of her eye she saw Henry sitting on a bench not too far away. Relieved, Vida walked towards him, but stopped at the look on his face, something was definitely wrong. His eyes, which were usually filled with warmth, were filled with fear for her. He was practically screaming at her to run silently. In a glance, she understood why. The pretty young girl sitting next to him with her purse in her hand had a gun pointed at him. She could see the girl's hand buried in the purse and the outline of the gun through the material pointed at Henry.

Vida started to turn and run, but stopped. She couldn't leave Henry to their mercy when it was her they wanted. If there was a chance for Henry to walk away, she had to give it to him and take a chance that King would save her.

She saw the anger in Henry's face directed at her as she

walked towards them, angry that she hadn't taken the opportunity to run.

When she drew close enough to hear her, the woman spoke.

"That black car over there, get in the backseat." The woman nodded to an inconspicuous dark car just a few feet away.

Vida nodded and started walking towards the car. As she came closer, the door opened from within and she hesitantly slid into the car. As soon as she shut the door, the car started and drove out into the busy street to be swallowed up in traffic.

"Is she going to let Henry go?" Vida asked, terrified for Henry.

The driver didn't respond to her question. Vida was frightened and couldn't stop her legs from trembling. She had no choice other than to lean back into the leather seats as she waited for the ride to end. When the car came to a stop, she became even more frightened when the driver got out and came around to her door. Opening it, he motioned for her to get out of the car.

The driver's cold expression left no doubt that she was in trouble. When the word trouble hit her mind, she was able to get herself back under control and hide the emotional turmoil that she was going through her. Stripping had taught her to hide her emotions, she needed that skill desperately now or the driver would be packing her into the house kicking and screaming.

Vida stepped out of the car, finding herself looking at a large home in an isolated area. Surrounded by a stone and metal fence, it was clear the owner wanted his privacy. She followed the silent driver into the house as he led her to a large room. As she walked into the room that held an expensive desk, a tall man rose from his chair and walked forward.

"Close the door, send in Briggs and Morgan." The driver closed the door, leaving Vida alone with the man staring back at her with malevolent eyes. He came closer, circling her as his eyes took in every aspect of her body. She felt as undressed as if she had been on stage at King's nightclub.

Stopping in front of her, his hand rose, backhanding her with such force her head snapped back, causing her to lose her balance and fall to the floor. Vida held her frightened cry inside, terrified that he would hit her again. Her shaking hand went to her burning cheek, hearing the door opening and closing, she looked towards the door to see Briggs and another man she recognized as Morgan from the club. She had performed lap dances for both of them. Neither of them acted like they had ever seen her before. No help would be coming from their direction.

"Get up, you stupid cunt."

Vida managed to get her feet under her and shakily rose up. The second time he hit her, she barely managed to stay on her feet, which was a mistake because his third hit was with his fist and sent her crashing back down to the floor. This time she was unable to keep her cries silent and she didn't try to get back up.

"You have been a pain in my ass for the last month. You should have stayed out of my business. Sawyer is mine, therefore she's my business." Laughing at his own joke, Digger leaned back against his desk, satisfied she wouldn't get up again.

"Briggs and Morgan tell me you can shake your tits and ass, so now you're my business," he informed her.

"King won't let you get away with this, I'm under his protection." Vida stared up at the ugly bastard who stood there as if he had the right to do anything he wanted.

"Fuck King, I'm not afraid of him. Has he managed to get Sawyer back?" Digger laughed sarcastically. "He couldn't even keep me from taking you from that stupid bodyguard. Take her up to my bedroom, I'll be up shortly." He went back behind his desk, sitting down to pick up a ringing cell phone.

Vida felt Briggs take her by the arm, helping her to her feet.

"Wait a minute, Briggs; put her on the chair. Seems like we have company." Digger put his phone back on the desk. Vida felt herself shoved down onto a chair in the corner of the room. Briggs stayed by her while Morgan stood by Digger. Vida noticed that Digger's countenance had undergone a change; she thought she caught a small glimpse of worry. The self-satisfied smile from moments before was gone.

Digger's driver, who no longer looked neat and refined, opened the door. Now, he was holding his ribs and his nose had blood dripping onto his white shirt. The man walking into the room wasn't any of the men she was expecting.

Colton strode into the room with an air of menace so visible that it frightened even Vida, who had had lived with him the last few weeks, unaware that he could be completely frightening when he was furious.

"Colton, I heard you were out of prison." The amicable tone coming from Digger had Vida's eyes turning back to him in surprise.

"Did you also hear Vida was living with me and was under my protection?" Colton's voice wasn't so amicable, in fact, in was downright threatening.

"Briggs might have mentioned it, but since you've been fucking anything that has a pussy since you've been out, I didn't think she was important."

"You thought wrong, Digger." Vida saw Colton take in her bruised face and blackening eye. His lips tightened and the air in the room turned more menacing.

"You hit her?"

"A mistake. Calm down, Colton. I apologize; I was misinformed as to her relationship with you." As Digger tried to excuse his behavior, she noticed Morgan's hand slip under his jacket.

"Come here, Vida." Ignoring Digger's excuse, Colton's

voice spoke over his.

She looked up at Briggs who didn't make a move to stop her. Slowly, still expecting him to prevent her from following Colton's order, she rose to her feet and walked to stand by his side. His hand reached out, smoothing her hair back into place. Taking her jaw in his hand, he turned her face to the side so that he could see the damage inflicted by Digger.

"You fucked up, Digger. You knew better than to touch something of mine," Colton threatened.

"I didn't know she was yours." This time the worry in his face became more pronounced.

"I was staying out of your disagreement with King, tried to show you respect, even though I knew it was undeserved, but I tried to give you—a former brother—leeway while King dealt with you. That is no longer the case."

"Colton, I don't want any trouble with you." Vida's head was spinning. Digger was afraid of Colton? He hadn't been afraid of King or his men, yet the obvious fear in his face showed that he hadn't wanted to antagonize Colton.

"You should have thought of that before you took her, much less laid your hand on her." Vida couldn't believe that she had thought at one time that Colton was afraid of Digger. Now that she had her eyes opened, she remembered that even King had spoken to Colton with mutual respect, not like he spoke to his men.

"A week, Digger. That's all I'm giving you to get Sawyer back here."

"That's not possible, Colton. She's out of my reach for the next three weeks. Obviously, I would get her back if I could to make amends, but it's impossible," Digger prevaricated.

Vida stiffened, about to demand that Sawyer be returned immediately when she felt Colton's hand on her arm. Looking into his tight face, she remained silent.

"Three weeks, Digger, not a minute more." Vida saw

Digger's eyes glance towards the security screens in front of him.

"Three weeks, she'll be here. Will that pacify the Predators?" Digger asked.

"For now. Don't disappoint me," Colton responded with cold finality.

"I won't," Digger stood up, coming forward as Colton turned Vida toward the door. His expression was ungracious. "I'm sorry, Vida. There was misinformation on my side. I would never have touched you had I known you were Colton's woman."

Colton's fist flew out, striking Digger in his lying mouth. Vida couldn't prevent the vindictive satisfaction she felt when she saw Digger almost lose his balance at the power of Colton's hit. Briggs and Morgan moved forward, but Digger motioned them back to their positions. Wiping the blood dripping from his mouth away with a handkerchief from his pocket, Digger didn't return Colton's aggressive move.

Colton walked to the door, holding on to Vida's arm, not worried about Digger attacking him while his back was turned. Vida couldn't help being amazed at Digger's deferential treatment of Colton. When they walked out the front door, Vida understood perfectly.

Well over a hundred motorcycles were on the yard in front of the house, parked everywhere. The manicured lawn with its pretty flowers was completely destroyed. Vida recognized one particular face towards the front of the pack.

Max got off his bike, crushing the few remaining flowers that had survived under his feet. Coming to stand in front of her, he took one look at her face and a furious look came over his features. He took a step towards the house, but Colton dropped his hand from Vida and held Max back.

"I already handled it, Max."

"Then I'm going to handle it some more. I'm going to

fuck him up." Max shook Colton's hand off.

"Max, we need him in one piece to get Vida's friend back, not with his mouth wired shut for the next few weeks. We'll handle him when she gets Sawyer back."

Max paused, looking down at Vida. "As soon as she's back, he'll regret ever touching you," he promised.

Vida stared at the group of men surrounding the house. "I think he already regrets it."

Laughter sounded from the rough looking men. Colton took her hand, leading her to his bike. Climbing on behind him, she held on to his waist as the men turned their bikes, driving out of the destroyed yard. Colton rode in the middle of the large group until they reached his apartment building. With a wave of his hand, he broke off from the pack. Colton then drove his bike into his parking spot, got off the bike and helped her off before turning to the four bikers waiting for his attention.

One biker was parked slightly ahead of the others. Colton grasped Vida's hand and led her to the man sitting casually on the bike.

"Vida, this is Ice, President of the Predators."

Vida didn't know how to react, so she gave him a smile and nodded her head.

"Vida? I like your nickname better." Ice gave her the once over before looking toward Colton. "Colton, you must be getting weak in your old age. If this pretty little bitch was mine, she damn sure wouldn't be putting those titties and ass out there for show." Watching Colton get reprimanded by a man who looked around the same age had Vida almost smiling. His hair was lighter than Colton's, but his attitude, while laid back, held a steely undertone of authority. Even if Colton hadn't told her he was the President of the Predators, his attitude would have given it away.

Colton stiffened. "She won't be any longer."

"I'm going to miss the show. Bring her around the clubhouse sometime," Ice invited. Vida tried not to blush when she realized Ice and the men behind him had seen her show. She recognized Max, whose bike was next to another biker. He gave her a wink.

Her eyes were drawn to the lone bike sitting further away than the rest. He kept Ice and the others within his sight, but continually surveyed everything going on around them. She had noticed several bikers through her lifetime; this one took dangerous to the next level. He wasn't good looking in the least; his face was too harsh. His features were actually handsome; it was what had been done to his face that had destroyed what, at one time, would have made women stop in their tracks. A scar ran the length of his face from his eye to just beside his mouth, giving his sensuous lips a cruel appearance. Vida's eyes were caught by his mocking green ones that were well aware she was staring at him.

"Go on up to the apartment. I'll be there in a minute," Colton told her, seeing her wince when she reached up to brush away a loose strand of hair.

Vida left, feeling the eyes of everyone on her back.

* * *

Colton turned back to the President of The Predators. "Thanks, Ice."

"No problem. Missed having you around the club the last three years." Colton and Ice stared at each other, both remembering their friendship and the fun they had partying together. "It's hard to think of Goldie's kid all grown up. She's a definite looker. Didn't make a move on her out of respect to Goldie."

Colton didn't say anything. Ice continued, "Hell of a situation you're in, man. Wouldn't want to be you." Ice started his bike. "Give me a couple days warning before coming by the club. I don't want to fuck with your parole. How long you stuck for?"

"One year."

"Fuck. It would kill me being away from the brothers that long. I hope this time you're smart enough to leave that bitch. I warned you from the beginning Tessa was bad news," Ice reminded him.

Every one of his brothers had tried to warn him about Tessa. He had listened, but hadn't played it smart. He had learned his lesson the hard way, in prison. If he got caught at the Predators' clubhouse, he could lose his parole and spend the last year of his sentence back in prison. He wasn't going to let that happen. More importantly, if he was seen there, it would open up the possibility of the club house being raided by the police, and he wasn't about to see his brothers suffer. He had lost the right to be a Predator when he had stepped forward and took the blame for Tessa's crime. Predators never got caught; they lived and breathed their motto.

"Already took care of it, two more weeks and the divorce is final," Colton explained to his former president.

Ice nodded. "Need anything?"

"No, I'm good. Thanks, Ice."

"Anytime, brother." Ice throttled his motor, driving the bike onto the road with the other club members following behind. Colton watched them leave until the last bike disappeared around the corner in the road.

Chapter Ten

Vida was sitting at the table with a baggie of ice against her swollen eye when Colton came in, slamming the door shut.

"What the fuck were you thinking?"

Vida stared at him in shock. She hadn't expected him to baby her, but she hadn't expected him to be so angry with her, either.

"What do you mean?" Vida asked, confused.

"I fucking mean, why in the hell would you get in the car in the first place. You should have run like the fucking devil was on your ass. They wouldn't have run you down on the campus."

"I was afraid they would shoot Henry," she explained.

"Again, a campus full of college kids. They would have had a SWAT team on them before they could have gotten away."

Vida began to feel stupid. "I didn't think."

"That's for damn sure. This whole situation you've put yourself in is one big fucking mess."

"I may have made a mistake with Henry, but the rest I have done what I had—" Vida tried to defend herself.

"No, Vida, what you should have done is what I told you to do long ago, and that was walk away," Colton interrupted.

Vida began to get angry herself. "I wasn't about to walk away from a degree that has been hard to earn. Plus, I will also be paying for it the rest of my life. I wasn't going to leave Sawyer behind, either; we made a pact. She worked a full time job then waitressed at night to pay the bills so I could finish school. We've saved and pinched every dime so that we would have enough cash to be able to go where we wanted. I am not fucking leaving without her!"

"I have news flash for you, Sawyer isn't fucking here. She's not here for you to leave behind. You're both going to be lucky if you don't end up buried next to your friend."

Vida sucked in her breath at his cruel words.

"You asshole. Don't you tell me what to do. The only thing you're attached to is your damn dick. You don't know what loyalty is; you fuck around on your wife. Not only do you fuck around on her, but you can't even fuck one woman, you fuck anything that moves and breaths in your direction." She had no qualms about showing her disgust.

"I haven't fucked you," Colton taunted.

"No, you haven't, because you are smart enough to know I don't want your skanky ass," Vida snapped back.

All the fear and loathing she had been holding inside for the last month was released into the harsh words she spewed towards Colton. She should have been thanking him for saving her from Digger, who had hit her and was obviously going to rape her before disposing of her. However, Colton's words about Sawyer and Callie had brought out the fight in her, which she couldn't get back under control.

"Is that so?" Colton questioned, his expression thunderous.

"Yes!" Vida spat back at him.

"Go get a shower. There's Ibuprofen in the medicine

cabinet; you're going to be sore later tonight. I'll fix us something to eat." Taking a deep breath, Colton managed to do what she hadn't been able to do. Reign in his temper.

Their argument ended so suddenly it took Vida several seconds to realize that Colton was no longer participating.

"I'm sorry, Colton. I didn't mean to fly off the handle. You were right; I shouldn't have gotten in the car. I didn't mean to snap your head off," Vida apologized.

"It's all right, Vida. Go get a shower." Colton didn't look back at her as he pulled cans out of the cabinet.

Vida felt terrible, yet went to take her shower. Taking clean clothes, she went into the bathroom. Turning the water on hot, she hoped it would take the soreness out of her body.

When she came out of the bathroom, she smelled hamburgers frying. Her stomach growled as she came to a stop in the kitchen. The waitress from the waffle house was back and she was standing at the stove frying the hamburgers. Colton was leaning casually against the counter. Talking to her, his face was relaxed and friendly with the woman fixing their dinner.

Vida felt a jab in her stomach. Refusing to admit she was jealous, she walked further into the room.

"Have a seat. Dinner will be ready in a minute." His friendly disposition changed when he saw her come into the room.

Vida sat down at the table, reluctantly feeling uncomfortable. Colton had never had a woman in the apartment outside of the bedroom.

He sat a plate down in front of her with the hamburger and a salad that she was sure Tammy was responsible for as well.

"Water?" he asked.

"Yes, thank you." Colton sat the drink down in front of her. Going back and forth, he sat a couple of bottles of beer down for Tammy and himself before sitting down on the other side of the table. Vida watched as he opened both bottles of beer and then handed one to the other woman.

She felt like a third wheel.

Tammy's gasp drew Vida's attention to find the woman staring at her in horror. "What happened to you?" she questioned, looking accusingly at Colton.

Colton had told her before not to break into his conversations, so Vida kept her mouth shut. Colton didn't seem pleased with Tammy's accusing look.

"Vida made someone angry that she shouldn't have," Colton informed Tammy.

Tammy didn't look as if her suspicions had been appeased. She cast looks back and forth between Colton and Vida. Colton gave Tammy a reassuring smile. When Tammy wasn't looking, Vida smirked at him. He began to look angry, which only fueled Tammy's suspicions.

"Stop it, Vida," Colton warned her.

Vida jumped in her seat and threw terrified eyes toward Tammy, all while managing not to burst out in laughter. The food tasted really good, despite watching Tammy flirt with Colton. She thanked Tammy, determined to hide how irritated she was becoming.

"It was delicious. I wish I could cook as well as you."

Tammy preened with the compliment from Vida.

"Let's go into the bedroom. Vida can do the dishes." Colton stood up, taking his plate and Tammy's to the sink.

Vida hastily stood, carrying her half-eaten plate to the counter. Taking an empty to go box out of the cabinet Vida put her half-eaten sandwich and leftover salad into it before putting it in the refrigerator. Tammy stood with her mouth open.

"We can't waste food." This time Vida wasn't joking when she saw Tammy's pitying look and Colton's angry one. The phrase coming out of Vida's mouth had obviously been droned into her by her quick response.

"I'm sorry, Colton, but I need an early night. I have to be at work early." Tammy went to the couch, picking up her purse.

"Tammy, she can eat whatever she wants. I don't starve her," Colton tried to explain.

Tammy looked at Vida's thin build and loose clothes.

"Honey, you get tired of his crap, I got an extra bedroom you can stay in until you get on your feet." Throwing Colton a look of disgust, she left in a whirl of perfume and high heels.

Vida waited until the door was closed before she broke down into laughter. She laughed so hard she had to hold her sides. Seeing Colton's smoldering gaze only set her off in fresh peals of laughter.

"I thought the black eye would do it..." Vida had to pause to catch her breath "...not the food. That's just habit. I guess she couldn't stand the thought of you not feeding her." Vida had to lean against the counter she was laughing so hard.

"Oh my God, your expression was priceless. And the madder you got only convinced her more that you were beating me."

Vida was so busy laughing she didn't notice Colton setting the dirty dishes in the sink or crossing the room to lock the door.

"Vida?" Colton's soft voice drew her attention as he now leaned against the counter with his arms crossed against his chest.

"Yes?" Vida wiped the tears of mirth away from her eyes.

"Do you know why I invited Tammy here?"

"Because you wanted to get laid." Vida didn't detect the danger she was in.

"Yes, because it was either get a woman here or fuck you. You have now taken that option out of my hands." Colton straightened, reaching for Vida. Sliding out of his reach, she thought he was paying her back for ruining his night.

"Don't take it so hard, Colton. Your next lay is only a

phone call away," Vida taunted.

"No, Vida. My next lay is six inches away." Colton strode forward. Belatedly realizing that he was serious, she took off running for the door. The doorknob was in her hand and she was pulling the door open when Colton's hand above her head slammed the door closed. Vida was held flat against the door as Colton's body pressed against her back and ass.

Vida stood still, realizing to late when she felt Colton's hardness against her backside just how serious he was about his intentions.

"What's wrong, Vida. Got yourself in trouble?" Colton whispered in her ear. His mouth nuzzled her neck, sending chills down her back.

"Let me go, Colton. I'll call Tammy and tell her I was just aggravating you."

"Too late. I didn't want her anyway. I want you. I was being nice keeping my hands off you. Since you don't want to play nice, I see no reason to continue fucking women that aren't you."

Vida tried to struggle free, however Colton held her still while his lips continued to explore her neck. He slightly lifted his weight off her and slid his hand across her midriff, seeking and finding the bottom of her top. His firm hand glided upwards across the flesh of her stomach, causing goose bumps to rise on her flesh.

His hand slid underneath her flimsy bra to find a nipple and begin twirling it between his fingertips. With Vida's hands against the door, she pushed back against him, but Colton forestalled her, widening his stance and using his other hand to grip her hip, pulling her ass back against his lengthening cock.

"You're making me so hard that I could come in my jeans." Colton's lips found her earlobe, gently biting it at the same time pinching her hard nipple. His hand then slipped from her breast, down her quivering stomach, his fingertips sliding underneath the fabric of her sweat pants.

"Stop, Colton!" Vida protested.

Colton took a step backward, releasing her. It took Vida several seconds to become aware he had released her. Turning from the door, she saw that he was standing by the couch, clenching and unclenching his hands.

"I stopped this time, Vida. Next time you play me like that, I won't."

"I won't. I'm not going to have sex with you, Colton," Vida told him bluntly.

"Five more minutes and I would have had you begging me." Colton's cynical voice had Vida's temper rising.

"I would never beg you, Colton. You take sex as seriously as chewing a piece of gum. You're married, and you're an ass." Vida raised her fingers counting off each one of his faults.

"You're a pain in my ass. I am not married. I told Tessa to get a divorce while I was in prison, she didn't. It will be final in a couple of weeks." Vida waited expectantly, but he made no excuses for being an ass.

"I'll move back into King's," Vida decided out loud.

Colton looked at her as if her intelligence was in question. "You move back in with King then Briggs will tell Digger. Next time he takes you, he will get you out of town so fast there won't be time to get you back before you're sold to someone."

Vida turned away, going to the closet to get her blankets and sheets. Making up the couch, she ignored him. Colton sighed and then left the room. Vida turned out the lights before lying down on the couch. Her body was sore and it finally hit her what Digger was going to do to her if Colton had not shown up. Moving restlessly on the couch, she was unable to get comfortable.

The nightmare came whenever she had an emotional upset. She had a recurrence for several nights after Sawyer's disappearance, but it had eased off. It came back with a vengeance now.

The dream began with flashes of her playing with

Sawyer and Callie, running down the halls and making everyone crazy. Then, the day gradually changed over to night in her dreams with the flames eating at her unconscious mind. She could still see herself screaming and knocking on Callie's door, the smoke pouring out from underneath. Her mom ran frantically toward her, picking her up and running down the hallway with her. Sawyer's mother was running in front of them, trying to escape the smoke filled hallway, her terrified eyes staring back at Vida had her crying in her sleep.

Vida felt cocooned in softness as her mother held her, rocking her gently then lifting her and carrying her to bed. She couldn't stop crying for Callie and Sawyer's grey eyes tormented her until she gradually managed to doze off with her mother gently stroking her hair.

Chapter Eleven

Vida tried to roll over and found herself pinned with an arm around her waist as well as a hard male body curved against her back. She stiffened, feeling a soft mattress underneath her. Trying to slide out from underneath the arm, Vida felt it tighten against her, pulling her backwards.

The arm turned her until she was lying on her back, staring up at Colton.

"Feeling better this morning?" Colton's thumb traced her black eye and bruised cheek.

"Yes, uh... how did I end up in here?" Vida asked, confused.

"You sleep walked in here and begged to sleep with me." Colton's straight face stared back at her.

"I did?" Vida's mind desperately tried to remember the night before. Colton's laughter brought her back, seeing him grinning down at her.

"You idiot." Vida hit him with her fists. Colton caught her hands in his then raised them above her head laying them on the pillow. Taking both her wrists into one of his, he laughed harder at her expression before becoming serious.

"You woke me up crying for Sawyer and Callie. I couldn't get you to stop crying so I brought you in here. It took awhile, but you finally managed to go back to sleep. You don't remember?"

Vida shook her head against the pillow. "All I remember is dreaming about the night Callie died."

"Poor baby." Colton's mouth dropped to nuzzle her neck.

"Colton, you can let me up. Don't you need to get to work?" Vida reminded him.

"In a minute." Colton raised his head, staring down intently into her eyes.

He lowered his lips until they rested gently against hers. Vida tensed underneath him.

"Relax," Colton murmured against her lips.

"I can't." Vida tried to turn her head away, but Colton took advantage of her parted lips, deepening the kiss.

His kiss went from gentle to firmly taking control as he slipped his tongue into the warm moistness of her mouth. As Colton explored her mouth, Vida gradually began to respond, pressing her lips back against his, her tongue seeking his.

His hands released hers, and at first, Vida didn't move them then she lowered them until they lay against his shoulders, trying to decide whether to push him away or pull him closer. However, Colton's tongue, thrusting in erotic movements, had her arms circling his neck and pulling him closer. Decision made as her fingers twined into his long hair.

Colton broke the kiss to glide towards her neck, taking detours here and there, exploring her soft flesh with nips and licks.

His chest lowered to hers, flattening her breasts against his chest. Her leg curled around his hip, pulling him against her. Colton took command, tilting her face back, his mouth returning to her lips, demanding more of a response from her. Vida almost baulked, but gave in to the pleasure of his heated kiss, becoming lost in passionate surrender.

His hand slid to her stomach and without hesitance slid inside her sweat pants. Vida felt his fingers glide through her moist cleft. Startled she tried to jerk her mouth and hips away, but Colton held her steady, his fingers not moving to enter her, only softly stroking to heighten her desire.

Vida was torn between wanting him to stop and for him to keep going. His fingers began rubbing her sensitive flesh harder, swirling the sensitive bud in a motion that had her jerking her hips, this time to follow his movements. Her leg wound around his waist harder. Small moans began to escape her mouth, which was trapped under his. Her hips wiggled closer towards his hard body that was pinning her down to the bed. A finger slightly entered her moist sheathe. Vida thought she would lose her mind at the pleasure when it sank deeper inside of her.

Colton raised his mouth from hers. Her passion glazed eyes closed at seeing the desire blazing from his eyes.

"What do you need, baby?"

"More," she said, unable to prevent the word from escaping her mouth.

"I can give you more." He inserted another long finger, keeping his palm pressing down on her clit. Vida began moving her hips back and forth, her hands grasping his shoulders. Her movements driving Colton's fingers higher inside her pussy.

His mouth went to her ear. "You're so tight. I can feel you're a virgin, Vida, right against my fingers." Vida felt his thumb slowly moving more seductively against her. "Have you ever let anyone play with this pretty, little pussy before?"

Vida tried to jerk her hips away, but Colton held her still with his chest and his palm pushing against her mound while his fingers kept up their torturous pumping.

"Answer my question." Colton's firm voice demanded

an answer.

"No," she said, trying to catch her breath.

"Your breasts? Have you let anyone suck on these pretty pink nipples?" he asked, nuzzling down into the gap her pajama top provided until he found her nipple, his tongued playing with it, turning the nub into a hardened point.

Vida moaned, wanting to stop, but also wanting more of him.

"You're going to like this, Vida. You're going to like this a lot." Colton's mouth latched onto her nipple while his fingers drove into her faster and faster.

Vida felt the pressure of a build up and slight pain with each thrust of his fingers as they butted up against her innocent flesh, until she was brought to a sudden climax. The spasms took control of her, forcing a shrill scream from her tight throat. Her body stiffened as she felt the loss of complete control to a pleasure she had never experienced before.

Colton rose above her, removing his hand from her warmth before pulling her pants back up and lowering her top until she was covered once again.

Vida lay stunned, wanting desperately to cry. She jackknifed straight up, startling Colton, and tried to jump from the bed. An arm around her waist stopped her, jerking her back as he leaned against the headboard and placed her effortlessly on his lap facing him.

"Where are you going?" Vida saw the amusement in his face, wanting to die of embarrassment.

"To the bathroom," Vida said in a strangled voice.

"You couldn't just tell me that instead of jumping out of bed like you saw a giant spider?" Colton looked at her quizzically.

"I need to go to the bathroom," Vida told him, trying to get off his lap.

Colton held her still with his hands on her hips. "In a minute." His hands slipped to her ass, adjusting her until he notched her pussy against his cock where thankfully, Vida noticed, he had on a pair of sweat bottoms.

She had a terrible feeling she didn't want to hear what he was about to say.

"Why are you still a virgin, Vida? No boyfriends in high school or college?" he questioned.

Vida was right; she didn't want to hear his questions, much less answer them. Her lips tightened.

"It's none of your business," she finally answered.

"Yes, it is, since I'm the one going to take it," he said casually.

"No, you're not," Vida snapped.

"Yes, baby, I am." He lifted his pelvis until she could feel his hard cock against her folds. Desire threatened to rise again and Vida felt herself begin to want him.

Vida shook her head. He was everything she didn't want in a man, everything she had sworn never to become attached to. Yet, he was sitting there, thinking he was going to take from her a gift that she had planned on keeping for someone special for years.

"No, you won't. I have saved myself for the man I fall in love with, which is not you, nor will it ever be you. I won't be like my mother, falling in love with one man after another, losing a piece of herself after each one. Do you know how many dads she brought home? Introduced me to? Each one she was sure was going to put that ring on her finger and make all her dreams come true. They never did, each one slept with her and used her until they were satisfied then they left her crying. She would cry for days, until she met the next one and fell just as hard.

"I am going to save myself for one man. A man who I know is going to love me as much as I love him, and won't leave me for the next piece of pussy he sees. He will be as committed to me as I am to him. That will not be you, you're a horn dog, and you're married!" she yelled.

Colton rose up from his relaxed position, bringing his chest against hers.

"The only man that is going to be between your thighs is me. I am going to take that sweet little cherry of yours and make it mine. You made yourself so many promises when you were a little girl there's no way you can keep them all. You're not a little girl anymore, Vida. You're a woman and you're going to want my cock in you. You're going to want it all the time." Leaning back against the headboard again, he gave her a tender smile. "If you're a good girl, I'll give it to you any time you want. If you're not, I'll make you beg for it." He gave her an arrogant smile that Vida had to restrain herself from knocking off him with the fist clenched at her side.

"You ass!" Vida moved to jump off him, and this time he let her go with a laugh.

"You better hurry up; we're late." Colton's voice followed her into the bathroom. She made sure to slam the door loud enough for him to hear.

Chapter Twelve

The tattoo shop managed to keep everyone busy, which made it easy for Vida to ignore Colton.

The door opening had Vida glancing up to see one of Colton's fuck buddies coming through the door.

"Does Colton have an opening?" she questioned.

"Yes, he does." Vida gave Tessa the client she had scheduled for Colton, penciling in Wanda for his next job.

"Have a seat; he'll call you when he's ready for you."

"Thanks." The girl smiled at her as she took a seat.

Tessa came out, ignoring Vida as she looked through the appointment book. Vida knew the exact moment Tessa noticed she had given her Colton's next client.

"Why did you give me Colton's client? I should have the client you gave him," Tessa questioned her sharply.

Vida pointed to Wanda. "She requested Colton. The client I gave you didn't. Colton said I should try to fill requests if it was possible."

"She requested Colton?" Her gaze sharpened on Wanda.

"Yes, she did." Tessa's face turned red as she snapped out the name of her client. She stood, talking to him about which tat he wanted for several minutes, her eyes never leaving the other woman who was becoming uncomfortable under Tessa's hateful glare.

Tessa gave the client directions to her room then walked over to Wanda. Vida sat, watching the oncoming confrontation, debating if she should get Colton to mediate.

"My husband will be with you in just a few minutes. He was almost done when I came out." Tessa's fake politeness didn't fool Vida, but it succeeded with Wanda.

"Your husband? Colton didn't tell me he was married."

Tessa smiled in satisfaction. "We've been married four years."

Wanda rose angrily to her feet, returning to the counter.

"Cancel my tattoo; I don't have the time to wait." Wanda left without waiting for a reply from Vida.

Tessa didn't try to hide the vindictive smile on her face as she left to finally get started on her waiting customer.

Colton and his client came out then, talking with Reverend.

"Did you take a picture of it? That one needs to go on the wall," Reverend said, taking a seat next to Vida.

"Took one in the room," Colton said absently, gazing down at the appointment book with a frown.

"Next time, Colton." The client waved as he left.

"Later, Kyle." Turning to Vida, he asked, "What happened to Wanda? I see her name marked out."

Vida shrugged innocently. "She waited for a while then said she couldn't wait any longer."

Reverend called his next client, looking at Vida and Colton quickly before escorting his client to his room.

Colton pulled out his cell, moving away from the counter as new clients came in the door. Vida fit them into the schedule, having to turn a few away for the moment and rescheduling those, while watching Colton as he talked on the phone. His expression becoming angry. He ended the call, striding furiously from the room.

Vida sat tensely behind the counter, becoming even more nervous when she heard raised voices from the back. A sudden loud noise sounded before Tessa came running out. Leaving the shop without a word.

The clients in the waiting area sat staring at one another until Colton returned.

"Who's my next client?" he asked grimly. Vida pointed to a heavyweight man sweating profusely. Colton called the man's name. She listened as the man described the tattoo he wanted that would take several visits. Colton led him away as Vida made future appointments to complete the desired tattoo.

Tessa reappeared with a cup of coffee, giving everyone the silent treatment for the rest of the day. Colton and Reverend worked without taking a break as Tessa got her revenge by taking huge amounts of time between clients. When the door closed at the end of the day, both men looked exhausted.

"You and Tessa need to get your shit straight, and you need to hire another artist. Word is out that you're out of prison. We can't do our best work if we keep pushing it with customers."

"I'll look around for another artist. The divorce will be final next week. Once Tessa realizes it's a done deal, she'll settle down or I'll fucking fire her."

Reverend looked skeptical, but didn't argue. "I'm going home to call a bitch to come and massage me down." Turning to Vida, he gave her a wink. "Unless you want to come home with me then I'll give you the massage."

"No, thanks. I think I'll just go to the apartment and fix dinner," Vida laughingly declined. "See you tomorrow."

Colton turned out the lights as Vida grabbed her backpack. Holding the door open, his eyes lowered, watching her walk toward him. Vida felt self-conscious as she walked to the motorcycle with him following, his gaze on her back. Putting on the helmet, she waited for him to get on before climbing on behind him.

Vida was surprised they were headed in the opposite direction of the apartment, wondering where he was headed. The sky darkened as Colton drove through town, eventually pulling into the driveway of a small house. Several lights were on, and a woman came out when she heard the bike's motor.

"Colton!" The woman threw herself into his arms. Colton laughed, picking the woman up and twirling her around in a circle before placing her back on her feet.

They drew apart and Vida was struck by the woman's resemblance to Colton. He placed a casual arm across her shoulder as he introduced her to the smiling woman.

"Vida, this is my sister, Brenley. Brenley, this is Vida."

"Hello, I can tell by your face that Colton didn't tell you he had a sister. He likes to surprise everyone that he actually has a family." Brenley made a face at her brother.

"I try to keep her hidden away. Everybody feels sorry for me that my sister's so ugly."

Brenley punched Colton in the stomach at his joke. Vida smiled as the two began to push and shove each other. She was amazed at this side of Colton.

"My big, ex-con brother is an embarrassment to me, too." She could dish it right back to her brother.

"Ouch, that's no fair. That's hitting below the belt."

"If I could have got to you before you made such a stupid move, I would have busted your balls," Brenley replied grimly.

"Well, it's over now and I'm home. What's for dinner? I'm starved." Colton changed the subject.

"I made your favorite; meatloaf." Vida saw Colton turn pale and Brenley snickered at him before leading the way into the house.

The aroma of fried chicken hit her nostrils as soon as she walked into the doorway.

"You witch. I'm not doing the dishes because you lied to me."

"You'll do the dishes or I won't cook for you anymore," Brenley threatened right back at her brother.

Colton made a face. "That's blackmail, but what can I do? I'm held hostage because you won't share mom's recipe book."

"If I gave you the recipes, I would never see you." Brenley's tone became more serious. "You two have a seat. Dinner's ready." The table was set for three people; Brenley had known that Colton was bringing her for dinner. Vida tried not to let warmth invade her at Colton introducing her to his sister.

"Can I help?" Vida offered.

"You and Colton can do clean up." Brenley smiled, setting down a platter of fried chicken before going into the kitchen and returning with potatoes and biscuits."

"I have died and gone to Heaven," Vida said, looking at the delicious food. Her mouth was watering from the aroma alone. Brenley laughed, placing a pitcher of tea on the table.

The talking stopped as they each filled their plates with the food that ended up tasting as good as it looked. Vida cleaned her plate, debating seconds, not wanting to make a pig of herself in front of Brenley. Colton demolished his food then had seconds. He seemed determined to eat everything on the table except the dishes.

"Slow down, Colton. I have plenty for you to take home for later," Brenley promised.

"It's been a long time since I ate food that tasted so good," Colton said when he finally finished.

Brenley smiled at her brother's compliment before getting up from the table and going into the kitchen with a wink in Vida's direction. She came back carrying a huge chocolate cake.

"Now, I have died and gone to Heaven," Colton sighed. Brenley cut each of them a big slice of the rich dessert. Even Colton couldn't manage a second slice.

After dinner, Vida and Colton both cleaned the table

and did the dishes while Brenley stood nearby, chatting with Colton and occasionally asking Vida a question.

Vida liked the woman, and finding out that she owned a small local business doing graphic designs only increased her admiration. Vida also enjoyed that her home was cozy and nicely decorated without being too girly. It was exactly what Vida dreamed one day of owning herself.

Deciding to watch a movie, they went into the living room. Brenley sat down in the only chair, leaving the couch for Vida and Colton.

Vida sat down on the end of the couch, however Colton eyed her before tugging her closer to his side. Embarrassed, she tried to scoot away a few inches.

Vida noticed Brenley's amused gaze on the silent struggle. Deciding it wasn't worth embarrassing herself, she stilled, relaxing into the sofa.

Colton leaned back, putting his boots onto the coffee table. Vida was about to take him to task when Brenley shook her head with a grin. Vida came to the conclusion that both brother and sister were used to getting their own way.

The movie was a comedy that had them all laughing. Vida wished it lasted longer when it went off and Colton pulled her to her feet.

"We'd better be going, Brenley. We have to work in the morning," Colton told his sister.

Brenley rose from the chair. "Let me get your leftovers." With a grin, she went into the kitchen.

"I like your sister," Vida remarked with envy in her voice.

Colton smiled. "She's pretty cool for a sister, but she can be a pain in the ass sometimes."

"I heard that. If you're not careful, I'll take that half of a chocolate cake out of the bag," she threatened.

"You're the best sister ever," Colton said soulfully. Vida laughed at his little boy act while Brenley handed him a plastic zip up bag that would make it easier to handle on the bike ride back.

"That's more like it," Brenley said before turning to Vida and giving her a quick hug. "It was really nice meeting you. Stop by sometime for a visit and I'll tell you all of Colton's secrets."

Vida couldn't help herself. "If it involves women, I think I'm finding that out for myself."

"I think the right woman could get Colton under control."

Colton took Vida's hand, leading her to the door. "Bye, sis."

"Bye, Colton. See you next week."

Colton tugged Vida out the door, hastily leading her to the bike.

"What's the hurry?" Vida asked, watching him strap down the food bag on the back of the bike.

"I didn't want my sister giving you more ammunition against me."

"I already know what kind of man you are, Colton."

"Do you? Or have you simply made judgments based on how I acted when I didn't care what you thought?"

Vida began to feel uncomfortable. She didn't want Colton's attitude to change towards her. She was comfortable with the way things were with them except for this morning, which she had every intention of forgetting about.

Without answering his question, she waited for him to get on the bike before getting on herself.

It had rained while they were inside, but the motorcycle drove effortlessly on the wet pavement. Colton was able to even control the bike when a car pulled out recklessly in front of them. Vida felt safe, not frightened in the least when she felt the bike's wheels slide slightly before Colton expertly maneuvered the bike to a slow stop. Expecting him to rant at the stupid driver, he surprised her by slowly regaining his speed until they were once more traveling through the night traffic.

She was becoming tired by the time Colton pulled up in front of his apartment.

"Mind if I take the shower first?" Vida asked once they were inside.

"No, you go ahead."

Vida didn't take long, wanting to go to sleep. Putting on her pajamas and brushing her hair before braiding it, she went out to the living room to see that Colton had made the couch for her.

Coming to a stop, she appreciated his thoughtfulness. She really didn't know how to handle this side of him. He had never been mean to her, merely treating her as a stranger in his home. Which she was. Now, with his change in attitude and how he treated her with consideration, almost like a girlfriend, she was beginning to be scared of the feelings it was bringing to the surface.

"Thanks, Colton." Vida stepped around him, moving towards the couch.

"No problem. I can see you're tired."

Vida lay down on the couch, already half asleep. Colton turned the light out when he saw she was settled. She was about to roll on her side when she felt him standing by her side.

"Colton…"

"I'm going to let you get used to the idea of us while I wait for my divorce." Sinking to the floor beside her, he reached out to cup her cheek. "When my divorce is final, Vida, you're going to be in my bed," he said firmly.

Vida was determined to shut him down before things could go any further. She was about to let him have it for his mistaken assumptions when his mouth closed over hers, his tongue driving all thoughts of denial away until he lifted his head, taking his mouth away from her and rising to his feet.

"Now you can go to sleep, if you can." Colton's thick voice had her wanting to drag him back.

Vida rolled onto her side, her body in turmoil and sleep

no longer close by. It took time for her body and mind to calm. Her body wanting his and her mind telling her to jump up and escape. Weariness finally overrode both, providing her with the sleep she needed.

Chapter Thirteen

Vida took a long time getting ready for work the next day, which provided her with the perfect excuse to ignore Colton. The morning ride to the tattoo shop had been full of nervous tension for her. Colton, on the other hand, was laid back as if he actually believed all he had to do was wait and she would fall in with his plans of having sex.

Vida didn't try to straighten his misconceptions out. She had plans of her own that didn't include an overconfident horn dog with the scruples of an alley cat. Vida's lips twisted at her comparisons, but they were the truth. Every woman that came into his shop was given the same gorgeous, seductive smile; they didn't stand a chance against his sexual chemistry that seemed to put them under his spell. Vida was going to be the exception, the one that could respite his fuck me smile. She took it as her personal mission to help these women fight back against his sexual allure, whether they appreciated it or not.

The shop was busy enough that with the extra part-time tattoo artist Colton had hired she could pick and choose which artist was given clients. It was easier to do with the appointments scheduled on the phone, but she learned a system of penciling in clients then erasing them and going over it in ink for the clients that came in the shop with nonscheduled appointments.

It took a couple a days before Colton became suspicious. By the fourth day, there was no doubt left in his eyes when he escorted his last client, a trucker who wanted a tattoo that would take at least a couple of hours. Vida gave him an innocent smile, but couldn't prevent the smile of satisfaction from her lips as Tessa's next client, who looked like a lingerie model and wanted a bunny tattoo, looked longingly at Colton as he left the room.

Later that evening, Vida powered down her computer, packing it away in her backpack, as she waited for Colton to clean his room so it would be ready for the morning. Colton drove everyone crazy on his habits of cleanliness, but Vida respected his concern for his clients.

"Did you lock the door?" Colton asked, coming in the room.

"Yes. Ready?" Vida stood up about to reach for her backpack.

"In a minute. Come back to my room. We need to have a talk."

"Can't it wait until we're back at the apartment?" Vida didn't like the grim expression on his face.

"No, it can't." Turning, he left the room while Vida followed reluctantly.

Entering the room, she saw he had his tray set out. She thought he would have put it away for the night.

"Have a seat."

Vida sat in the chair he used to tattoo his clients.

"Ever wanted to get a tattoo?"

Vida, expecting him to take her to task for the clients he had been given, was surprised into giving an honest answer.

"Yes."

"Why haven't you gotten one?"

"I really don't know. I couldn't make up my mind

which one to get or exactly where I wanted one."

"Trust me?"

"Yes." Vida had seen his work since she had started at his shop and it was really good.

"Then, you're getting your first tattoo."

"My first? I only want one," Vida objected.

"Nobody has just one tattoo," Colton said absently as he pushed the stool closer to her. Moving her top to the side, he took a cloth and wiped where she thought he planned to put her tattoo. Vida stared ahead as he began to work on the front of her shoulder next to her collarbone.

"I will," Vida said adamantly.

"We'll see." He continued to work on her. It wasn't as painful as she thought it would be, but was glad it wasn't overly large. She kept trying to look down to see what he was doing.

"Stop it, or your lines are going to be crooked." Vida stopped moving, straightening in the chair. "The shop's been busy this week," Colton said matter-of-factly.

"Yes, more money for you and your partners." Vida joked half-heartedly, dreading where this conversation was heading.

"Yes, it is." He swiveled on his stool and then dunked his needle in ink before swinging around to begin drilling into her again. "You doing okay?"

"Yes."

"I noticed something a little strange this week." He continued to work steadily.

"Oh really?" Vida tried not to look down at what he was doing.

"Um, hm."

"What did you notice?" she asked when he didn't continue. Her nerves were stretching to a breaking point.

"I have had three women this week. Two that are happily married, and one that wanted her wife's name on her arm."

"That's so sweet."

Colton paused, looking up at her with narrowed eyes. "Yes, it was. Can you explain how I had such an overabundance of male customers when I saw several female clients in Tessa, Reverend's and Carlito's rooms?"

"Luck of the draw?" Vida pretended to stare at one of his drawings on the wall.

"If you give me another trucker that hasn't bathed in a week, or a businessman who wants a pussy tattoo without it being my turn again, I'm going to turn that ass up and smack it until you can't sit down."

Vida swallowed hard. "I didn't—"

"Yes, you did. Don't deny it." Colton didn't look up at her, merely continued working, wiping her shoulder off. He slid his stool back. "You're done."

Vida got out of the chair, going to the mirror to look at her new tattoo. Staring, she was tempted to touch it, but didn't. If was a beautiful butterfly. Its fragile, colorful wings were captured in whirls of lines and colors.

"Thank you, Colton. It's beautiful."

"Glad you like it. Now let's go home." He put his equipment up after cleaning his station while Vida admired how professional he was, and surprisingly meticulous.

"Let me wrap it." Vida turned back to him as he placed a wrap on her tattoo. "I'll put some lotion on it later. Make sure you don't get it wet when you shower."

"I won't." Vida nodded happily at the same time that Colton smiled indulgently.

Turning of the lights in his room, they closed the shop and drove home. The night air on his bike always refreshed her, but much too soon, they were at his apartment.

Vida went to the kitchen to fix them something to eat. By the time Colton got out of the shower, Vida had fixed them chicken and rice. She had discovered both of them had big appetites, but didn't like cooking. To stay fair, they took turns cooking.

They ate while Vida questioned Colton how he had

began tattooing.

"I always liked to draw and was really good at it. In the Predators, one of the brothers was a tattoo artist. He gave me my first tat then, seeing I was interested, took me on as an apprentice."

"You're really good," Vida complimented. "Do you miss not being in the Predators?"

"Yes, they became my family. My dad took off when I was ten-years-old and never came back. Mom remarried; he was cool, but I could tell he wanted Mom to himself." Colton shrugged, taking the dirty dishes to the sink before grabbing a beer from the refrigerator and sitting back down at the table. "So when I was sixteen, I started hanging out at the Predators' clubhouse."

"Your mom didn't mind that you were hanging out with outlaw bikers?"

"No, because my stepdad was a Predator."

"Oh." Vida didn't know what to say. She couldn't ever imagine willingly letting a child of hers become involved in a motorcycle club.

"They're not all bad, Vida. The Predators are loyal. Their activities may not be completely legal, which is why the brothers can't let me visit without notice. If I'm around drugs, guns or convicted felons, I could lose my parole."

"I'm not going to say anything negative about them, Colton. They helped save me from Digger, and if they scare him enough to get Sawyer back, I'll owe them a big favor."

"Don't tell them that or you'll be giving private performances for the brothers at the clubhouse," Colton said seriously. "I'll handle any gratitude they have coming."

Vida packed her own dishes into the sink and then filled it with hot water. "You going to strip for Ice?" Vida teased.

The dishes didn't take long, Colton sat at the table until she finished.

"I think I'll take my shower." Vida didn't want to sit

and watch TV with him as she had the last few nights. She was beginning to look forward to spending time alone with him now that he was opening up, telling her about his past and drawing her closer to him.

Vida couldn't let herself get attached to him. She kept telling herself this over and over, remembering her mom after each and every one of her relationships had ended. Colton was more of a horn dog than any guy her mom had dragged home.

She showered, careful to keep her tattoo dry, and when she finished, she dressed in pajama pants and a top. After brushing out her long hair before she braided its thick length, she exited the bathroom to find Colton waiting for her.

"I need to rub some lotion on your tattoo and rewrap it. Have a seat on the couch."

"Okay."

Colton sat down on the couch, waiting expectantly. She sat down next to him, reaching up to tug her pajama top to the side, but Colton forestalled her by reaching out and casually unbuttoning her top and sliding it off her shoulder.

"What the hell?" Vida screeched, trying to pull her top back up.

"Stop it, Vida. Don't be ridiculous. You do realize I saw your strip act. Not only that, but I've had your nipples in my mouth." Vida didn't appreciate being reminded of him seeing her naked.

Gently, he unwrapped her tattoo.

He grew tired of her fidgeting with the top. "Sit still, Vida."

Vida pulled her top up to cover her breasts, making herself sit still as he rubbed lotion onto the tattoo before rewrapping the sensitive skin. When he was done, he tugged her top from her hands, helping her to slide her arms back into the sleeves. Before she was able to button it up between her breasts, he held the material apart as his knuckles stroked the soft globes.

Colton leaned forward to kiss the flesh between her breasts. Then, without rising up, he brought his weight forward. Vida leaned backward, trying to move away only to find herself lying on the couch with Colton above her. His lips traced towards a pink-tipped nipple. Laving it with his tongue, he surrounded the tip with his mouth and then sucked her into the erotic heat of his passion.

Vida's head moved against the couch as he played with one breast before turning to the other, giving it the same tormented attention. All of Vida's good intentions disappeared as her insides clenched in need. She knew her body was telling her it wanted him; the warmth between her thighs was burning her, wanting instinctively to be filled.

Colton's mouth moved away from her breast, downward across her stomach, teasing her belly button while making her stomach muscles quiver. Colton tugged her pajama bottoms off, letting them fall to the floor. Vida tried to slide out from underneath Colton, having no intention of having sex with him, but Colton used the opportunity of her movements to slide down between her thighs.

"Colton, I'm not sure—"

"I know, baby. I'm not going to fuck you tonight. I'm just going to make you want me to."

Colton's mouth covered her pussy, consuming her in a fire she had never experienced before. His tongue slid between the cleft, finding her clitoris. Vida lost what little restraint she had left; her hips surged forward, trying to seek pressure against her where she needed it the most, instinct driving her movements to seek relief. Colton eased his tongue along the tip of her passage, exploring the delicate flesh. She twisted not wanting gentleness, instead she wanted something to ease the building desire.

He used his finger to trace the fleshy side of her pussy. "I'm going to tattoo my initials right here."

"No."

"Yes. Right... here." He touched a spot to the side of her mound. "This pussy is going to be mine, only mine, Vida. Do you hear me?"

"I'm not going to let you tattoo your initials down there. It would hurt like hell!" Vida protested, shocked.

"Baby, when I tattoo you there, you won't even feel it." Colton promised with a wicked grin before he lowered his mouth to her once again.

Vida tried to regain control of her body, but she was weak against the experience he used against her. His teeth tantalized her flesh. He even used the piercing under his bottom lip to brush against her, causing a storm of sensations she recklessly let herself enjoy before it escalated into a need that had her hands drag through the length of his hair, forcing him against her as she tried to seek the orgasm he was denying her.

Vida began to plead with him. "Colton..."

"Do you want me, baby?" Colton asked against her moist flesh.

"Yes." Vida knew he was waiting for her to give in, but didn't care anymore. She wanted her aching body to be given the satisfaction she knew he was capable of giving her.

Colton sat up, pulling her up with him. Reaching down to the floor, he picked up her pajama bottoms. Vida stared at him stupidly as he helped her put them back on before pulling her pajama top up and buttoning it to her throat.

"I don't understand." She saw Colton wince as he stood to his feet.

"I wanted to give you a little taste of what you say you don't want."

"You were teaching me a lesson?" Vida asked, her body hurting.

"Baby, are you ready to be in my bed every night? Have me fuck you anytime I want?"

Vida didn't answer.

Colton grinned, bending down to kiss her mouth. Vida's lips parted, letting his tongue enter her mouth and stroke hers in a voracious kiss. Pulling away, he straightened to stand above her, his hand going to her braid where he tugged it until she stared helplessly up into his hard face.

"I'm trying to give you time, Vida. I want you to admit that there's something going on between us. I want you to want me to fuck you as much as I want to," he explained bluntly, bringing out in the open what Vida was trying to ignore.

Vida winced at his crude words.

Colton sighed, squatting down in front of her, he put his hand on her cheek, his thumb caressing her soft skin.

"I'm not a hearts and flowers kind of guy. You mean something to me, Vida."

"I don't want to mean anything to you. I don't want you to mean anything to me. I have plans. I want a home and a life, like your sister."

"Do you plan on living that life alone or are you going to share that life with a man, children?" Colton asked, his face gentle.

"Of course."

"Then why can't it be me?" Vida turned her eyes away at his prying question.

"Because you've been married. You aren't faithful to her. You expect her to be around you and not care that you're with other women. I've seen how you treat women, Colton. You use them for sex then don't call them again." All her fears of him being like the men that used her mother came out in her words.

Colton sighed again, this time deeper. "I really have gotten off on the wrong foot with you." Colton rose to his feet. "Vida, I'll tell you about my marriage soon, but not late at night when you're tired. I will say that I went into my marriage wanting it to work out, and when it ended, it ended badly for both of us. That doesn't mean that a relationship with us couldn't work, that I wouldn't be good to you. I would be very good to you, baby." This time his thumb rubbed over her bottom lip.

"How about we take it one day at a time and get to know each other better until my divorce becomes final?"

"What about when your divorce becomes final?"

"Then all bets are off. I'll take you to my bed, and you can get to know me even better." He smiled at her wickedly, rising to his feet. "Lie down."

Vida lay down and Colton spread out a blanket on top of her. Giving her a gentle kiss with a sweet "Goodnight" against her parted lips, he left her tired and confused about his treatment of her.

He could be so domineering and arrogant, yet he had reassured her and made her feel wanted and desired as well.

He had let her know he had every intention of having sex with her and confirmed her worst fear that emotionally they were growing closer.

Confused, Vida stared at the dark ceiling, her mind in turmoil and her body still desperately wanting Colton.

Chapter Fourteen

Vida dressed in loose jeans and a pretty red top that had capped sleeves, her tattoo looking pretty against the bright color of her top. Brushing her hair, she pulled it back from her face with two combs, but left the long length down her back.

"You look fucking gorgeous," Colton complimented when he saw her. A blush rose in her cheeks. He had a way of making her feel feminine and sexy with simply a look from his eyes, however he didn't try to hide the dirty thoughts going through his mind.

Vida shook her hair back. "How does it look?"

Colton's gaze didn't go to her tattoo as she had intended, but to the cleavage her top exposed. He opened his mouth to reply.

"I meant the tattoo."

Colton closed his mouth. "Let me rub some more lotion on it before we go. It looks good on you. I do good work."

"Yes, you do," Vida complimented.

Colton rubbed the lotion on the still tender skin. His knuckles brushed the tops of her breasts before stepping back.

"We better go, or we're going to be really late." His tight jaw left no doubt what activity would delay them.

They stopped for breakfast at a waffle house on the way to the shop. Colton chose a different one than the one Tammy worked at, which was close to the apartment. Vida didn't question his choice, merely giving him an amused grin.

Enjoying herself, Vida found herself relaxing even more in his company as he told her stories about when he first joined the Predators and their exploits to embarrass the new recruit.

She laughed until she was almost crying when he described standing watch over a dumpster that the brothers told him had a money drop in it until someone came to retrieve it. When the brothers came back to pick him up and he told them no one had showed, he had to jump in the dumpster to retrieve the drop bag. It hadn't been easy to find and was outside in an alley that had several restaurants. He had described how he had almost vomited several times, only the humiliation he would suffer if he had, had him choking it down. When he had finally found the bag, they had told him to open it. Inside the bag, he told her, they had placed his cut. They had made him a member, and he had passed his final test. Of course they had made him walk back to the clubhouse, as no one wanted to ride double with him.

"I can see why you miss that life," Vida teased. "Gives you an excuse to go dumpster diving."

"When we have time, I'll tell you some stories of what I used to pull on the recruits," he bragged.

"Worse than dumpster diving?"

"Much worse," he confirmed.

Vida climbed on the back of his bike, laughing at his dire voice.

The ride to the shop didn't take long, both of them walking into the shop with smiles on their faces. Tessa stood behind the counter with the appointment book in her hands, eyes narrowed on them in suspicion.

Vida ignored her, letting Colton deal with the temper she could see brewing. She was not able to prevent herself from feeling guilty when she remembered she was his wife, however close to a divorce they were.

"I was wondering when you were going to show," Tessa said snidely.

Colton gave her a sharp look; Vida could tell he wasn't happy with her sharp tone of voice.

"I'm not late. In fact, my first client isn't scheduled for another thirty minutes."

Forestalled in her effort to find something to rip into him for, her eyes fell onto Vida's tattoo. "When did you get that tattoo?" Her eyes bore into it.

"Colton did it last night after the shop closed." Vida tensed, seeing from Tessa's face going pale that something was wrong. Her eyes turned to Colton, shocked to see apprehension instead of the anger she expected.

"You gave her your symbol, but never tatted one on me, even though you gave me three fucking tattoos."

Colton didn't reply.

"I don't understand. What symbol?" Vida stared back and forth between the two.

Tessa swung back to Vida. "Are you fucking blind?" Tessa pointed to the butterfly. "He's fucking telling everyone that you're his." Vida looked down at her tattoo, not seeing anything other than the butterfly.

"She can't see it. Even if she looked in a mirror the lines would be reversed," Colton explained.

Vida began to get angry. "What did you do?" Her voice had sunk to a whisper.

Tessa's hand pointed to the pictures that hung around the lobby. "Look how he signs his pictures."

Vida got up from the desk and took a closer look at the pictures hanging on the wall. Each one was signed with a symbol, which blended the initials of his first and last name together.

"Why would you do that?" Vida questioned him angrily.

"Wanted to make sure that everyone knew you were mine. Anyone that knows tattoos will easily see that those are my initials."

"You might as well have his name tatted on your shoulder." Tessa swung back to Colton. "How many times did I ask to put your name on me? You told me no." Tessa's hand reached out and snatched up the stapler, throwing it at Colton who didn't move out of the way, but caught it in his hand.

"Do you really want to go into this in front of Vida?" Colton never lost his cool, even when Tessa threw the stapler at him. Vida was surprised; she had thought that Colton would be the type of man who would react physically when challenged like Tessa had by being the first one to try to get physical.

"I don't give a fuck what she hears," Tessa screamed at him.

"I tatted your name on me several time's, I told you I would be faithful, be committed to our marriage. You were committed to one thing; the snow you shoveled up your nose. You know why I didn't put my name on you? You thought I would forgive and forget. I can't forgive you for what you did. You lied to me straight out about how much you were using, then I caught you stealing from the shop. And when I thought you were doing better controlling your habit, you were selling your pussy for Digger to keep you in your habit. Everyone in this town knew except me that you were fucking around on me. Then, the night I got busted by the cops, King told me everything, and every dirty little detail your life had become." Colton's words were painful for Vida to hear. She had been wrong to assume the failure of his marriage rested on his shoulders.

"Then why did you keep me out of prison?"

"Because you were carrying my kid, Tessa."

Vida stiffened in her chair. Seeing the pain on Colton's face, she knew that she didn't want to hear anymore, but she was trapped, not wanting to draw attention to herself by getting up.

"King called me when he heard from his informant on the police force that the bust was going down. He told me everything that was going on behind my back. You had told Digger you were pregnant, but not me." Colton paused before continuing in an emotionless voice.

"I wasn't going to have my pregnant wife in prison delivering my baby. So I took the blame, and you got rehab." Tessa had taken a step back as if struck when Colton had mentioned the baby.

"Colton, I was going to tell you," Tessa tried to explain, but Vida could tell it was too little too late.

"When were you going to tell me, Tessa? You never mentioned in all this time that you were pregnant. If one of King's women hadn't overheard you telling Digger, I would have never known. When I went in prison, a couple of the brothers kept an eye on you for me, that's how I found out you aborted my baby."

"Colton, I was doing so much coke. I was messed up. I figured I had damaged the baby so bad that—"

"Shut up, Tessa, or so help me God, I'll hurt you."

Tessa shut up. Vida heard Colton take a deep breath, trying to regain control.

"So, no, I didn't want my name inked on you to remind me every fucking day how stupid I was to marry you in the first place. I called you every month while I was in prison, serving your time, to get the divorce. When you didn't, I handled it, but you wouldn't even show me the respect to sign your fucking name to the papers."

Colton nodded his head towards Vida. "She doesn't think I can be a faithful because I fucked so many women when I got out of prison and was still married to you, when the truth of the matter is, our marriage ended the first time you spread your legs for a dime bag of coke."

Vida saw Tessa swipe away the tears on her face.

"Now, can we get to work before the clients start coming in and someone else hears my private shit?"

Reverend and Carlito came in the door, both coming to a stop when they saw everyone look their way.

"What's up?" Reverend said into the tension-filled silence of the room.

Colton and Tessa remained silent.

Vida spoke up, trying to get the day back on track. Opening the schedule book, she read off everyone's first appointment. "Carlito, you're first up for walk-ins."

"Cool, they end up being more fun." Carlito was a good-looking man of Mexican descent who didn't let anything faze him. Vida had talked to him several times when he was between customers. He would sit at the desk beside her, playing on her computer.

The clients began arriving, so the artists and clients moved off to their respective rooms. Thankfully, after the rocky start, the shop was busy keeping everyone occupied. Tessa remained quiet when she would venture into the lobby to greet her customers, not even looking at Vida who felt uncomfortable after hearing the details of Colton's and her marriage.

Vida didn't know how she felt. She was angry that Colton had tattooed his symbol into her butterfly, but at the same time, she felt a sense of belonging that she hadn't experienced since her mother's death. She refused to dwell on it until she was able to talk to Colton about it tonight. She had been scheduled to perform at the Strip club for the last time, but Colton had called and cancelled for Vida after Digger had promised to return Sawyer. King hadn't protested, relieved that his part in retrieving Sawyer was no longer necessary.

Vida glanced up when the door opened and Seth entered, wearing a sheepish expression on his face.

"Hi, Vida."

"Seth." Vida's voice was cool. The hurt she had

experienced when he had left after learning she was a stripper was evident.

Vida watched as he blushed at her cool reception.

"I know you're angry, Vida, but I'm hoping we can go out to lunch and talk, please. We don't have to go far, just across the street. I'd like to explain." Seth's apologetic gaze had her hesitating in giving her refusal. She had liked Seth and thought they had become friends. She hadn't thought that he would have been the type to turn his back on someone because they might not live up to his standards.

"I don't know," Vida tried to prevaricate.

"Please, Vida. If not lunch, then how about a cup of coffee? My treat. I really would like to explain why I was a jackass."

"Let me tell Colton I'm leaving for lunch," Vida gave in.

Carlito, escorting his customer out of his room, said he heard her. "I can watch the desk. I'll tell Colton when he comes out."

Vida hesitated, thinking she should tell Colton, but knew he didn't like to be interrupted during a session. "Okay. Thanks, Carlito."

Vida and Seth walked across the street to the coffee shop where Vida sat at the table while Seth braved the long lunch line to get them a couple of coffees. Vida wasn't hungry and didn't want to be away from the shop too long. Something told her Colton wasn't going to be too happy to learn that she had left the safety of the shop to be alone with Seth. She actually wasn't too certain it was a smart idea herself.

Seth sat down across from her, giving her the cup of coffee she had asked for with packets of sugar.

Vida took a drink of the sweet coffee, looking over the brim of the cup at Seth who was staring at the customers sitting at tables surrounding them. He looked back, catching her eyes on him. He seemed different since leaving the shop. More assured and confident, his shyness was gone and he was meeting her gaze directly.

The cautious feeling Vida had was becoming a definite twinge of fear as she could see the dramatic change in Seth.

"Don't be afraid of me, Vida. I'm here to help you." The self-assured voice trying to calm her was a far cry from the diffident tone she usually heard from him.

"How can you help me, Seth?" Vida tried to loosen her tight grip on her cup, afraid she was going to burn herself if she wasn't careful.

"I'm an undercover agent, working to get back Sawyer and several other women like her that have been taken against their will." Seth reached into his pocket and as best he could, without drawing attention to what he was doing, showed her his badge.

"You're with the FBI?" Vida stared at him in disbelief.

Vida couldn't believe that Seth was a FBI agent. He looked like he was still in high school.

"The FBI has been trying to shut down Digger for years. Every time we get close, he manages to wiggle his way out of it or get information he's about to be arrested, and moves the women to another location. He's responsible for a pipeline, not only of illegal drugs, but he also uses that same route to sell women."

Vida was sick to her stomach that she was ever in the vicinity of the man that Seth was discussing, becoming even more thankful to Colton and the Predators for saving her.

Seth leaned closer, lowering his voice. "We're getting closer. We managed to shut down his informant on the force so, if we could find the location where he's keeping the woman, we can get a conviction this time."

"Thank God."

"That's why they wanted me to make friends with you. To find out what you and King know. The day in your shop, I recognized the friend of Colton's that came in. I think I got out of there before he recognized me, but I don't know. Max is a hard ass and not much gets by him. After I talked to the task force, we decided it was worth letting you know about the operation so that we could ask for your help in finding the women."

"Me? How can I find out where the women are? I really, really don't want to play bait and have you following me. I don't think those scenarios turn out too well."

Seth laughed while still retaining his serious expression. That convinced Vida more than his badge that he was telling her the truth.

"You've been watching too much television. I wouldn't place your safety in danger to that extent. What we need from you is to do what you have been doing until recently, go to King's and try to get what we need out of Briggs."

"How do you know what I've been doing with Brigg's?" Vida's asked.

Seth remained quiet, taking a drink from his coffee.

Realization dawned on Vida.

"You have King's place bugged?"

"I can't reveal how we know what you've been up to, only that we know. It's because of your prying that we've learned as much as we have."

"I was scheduled to dance tonight, but Colton cancelled with King."

"We know. That's why we want you to call King and tell him that you want to work tonight. Briggs is expecting you there, and after they kidnapped you, he's going to try to convince you to trust him. We're hoping he tries to convince you by letting a little too much slip with your probing," Seth said tactfully. Vida understood that his tact with using "probing" actually meant "while you're grinding your ass on his lap".

"I'll tell Colton…"

Seth shook his head. "No, he has several connections that aren't trustworthy. If he isn't careful, he could let information out that leaks back to Digger. Digger has a few friends left in the Predators, not many, but a few that would warn him. You've managed, hopefully, to get Sawyer back, but you don't know for sure. This gets us closer and will help those women that aren't ever going to get found without your help."

Vida only had one recourse, and that was to do as he asked. She wouldn't be able to live with herself if Sawyer wasn't returned, and she had an opportunity to help other women in the same horrific situation.

"I'll help, but I don't know what I'll tell King or Colton," Vida agreed.

"Think of something, anything, but keep the focus off Briggs," Seth told her.

"All right, I'll do my best. I better get back," Vida said, standing up.

"Thanks, Vida. You have my number if anything happens, and if you need my help, just call. Be careful. Don't underestimate, Briggs. He's as dangerous as Digger." His warning had her pausing at the concerned look on his face.

"I know." Vida still remembered Briggs's reaction when Digger had told him to take her to his bedroom. He had planned to use her also.

Vida shuddered at the lucky escape she'd had. Sawyer hadn't been so fortunate. Vida prayed against all odds that whoever had her wasn't treating her badly.

Vida crossed the street, leaving Seth at the coffee shop while she tried to decide what to do because she was afraid that, if she chose wrong, Sawyer's life would be the price of her failure.

Chapter Fifteen

Colton was staring out the window when she entered the tattoo shop, making no pretense that he had been watching her, or that he was angry with her.

Taking her arm, he led her into his room and then closed the door.

"What were you thinking of leaving the shop without telling me? One of Digger's men could have grabbed you." His hard voice left no doubt in Vida's mind of his concern for her safety. It convinced Vida of what the best course of action she should take.

"Colton, calm down. I need to tell you something." Quickly as possible, she told Colton about her conversation with Seth, including the part about Digger still having friends in the Predators.

Colton sat down on his stool, deep in thought. "He's right, I know of a couple and a few more might even be in with him and are just playing it cool so that no one knows of their involvement with Digger's activities. The Predators are not exactly law abiding, but they don't go for selling women against their will."

"What should I do? I don't want to jeopardize Sawyer's

safety, but I can't simply not help those other women, either."

"Did Seth say my shop is bugged?" Colton asked.

"I didn't think to ask," Vida confessed, angry with herself.

"I don't think it is, but I don't want to tip the FBI off to what we're going to do."

"What are we going to do?"

"Talk to King." Colton wrote the words down on his drawing pad. Vida agreed. King had offered his help before anyone else, including the police.

"Go back out front," he said while he continued to write. "I'll call King and set up a meeting," he wrote.

Vida started to open the door, but Colton's voice had her pausing and looking back towards him.

"Don't go off alone again, Vida." Hearing the threat in his voice, she nodded her agreement before slipping out the door and closing it behind her.

The rest of the day was slow. Tessa and Carlito left early when no other clients came in and they had finished with their scheduled appointments.

"Let's go." Colton was leaning against the counter. "Reverend said he would close up the shop."

Vida rose from her chair when Tessa came back in the door. They both tensed, expecting the woman to pick up where the argument ended this morning. Instead, she walked directly to Colton and handed him a sealed envelope.

"I signed the divorce papers. I took them by your lawyer's office. That's a copy of them." Her face was expressionless, but Vida could tell by the pain in her eyes how badly she was hurting.

Colton's hand gripped the envelope. "Thanks, Tessa."

Tessa shrugged. "It's obvious you're moving on with several women." Turning around, she left them, leaving them in the silence of her sudden departure.

Vida started to say something then closed her mouth,

not knowing exactly what to say. The end of a marriage was never a good thing. It was the ending of a dream that two people shared in that moment, Vida could tell that Colton had cared for Tessa at one time and had tried to save his marriage. He'd even gone to prison, still trying to hold it together and protect his child.

Vida came to the conclusion in that moment that he wasn't like the men her mother had attached herself to. Colton, when he had decided to marry, had committed himself and given it every chance. It was Tessa who, despite her last harsh words at parting, had turned her back on their marriage.

Colton unlocked the apartment door, holding it open for Vida to enter. Vida came to a standstill when she saw King sitting on the chair in the room.

Colton's brow rose as he came in the door, closing it behind him.

"How many keys to this apartment are floating around?" he asked King.

King gave him a smile. "I didn't use a key."

"Figures, you might not want to draw attention to your talent of B and E with the cops listening in to your every move."

The smile disappeared in a flash. "What do you mean by that remark?"

Colton and Vida both sat down on the couch and went over the talk that Seth had with Vida earlier in the day.

Vida watched as King's impassive face turned angry when he found out his club had been bugged and was under police surveillance.

"What do you think we should do?" Vida asked before he could become too angry, wanting him to focus on how to keep Sawyer safe. King rose from the chair, going to the window and staring out for several minutes before turning back to them.

"I'm afraid they're right. The only way to stop Digger is to let the FBI have him." King put his hands in his pockets and stared at Vida. "Looks like Trouble will be taking the stage one last time."

Vida looked unhappily back at King. She had known all along it was the best course of action to take, but it wasn't going to make it any easier going on that stage to perform.

"Do you think Briggs will slip up?" Vida asked.

"I don't know. He's pretty loyal to Digger," Colton told her.

"Let's see if we can't help that along then. He likes to drink while he watches you on the stage. I'll make sure his glass doesn't stay empty, so that, by the time he gets his lap dance, he might not be in a clear-headed frame of mind." King plotted Briggs's downfall.

"That might help. You could also get a couple of the shot girls to pay him some extra attention, have him worked up." King's mouth twitched into a grin at Colton's suggestion.

"How are you going to keep him under control when you want to get away? The worst thing you could do is let him know he slipped up, and realizing it when one of the men have to pull him off you," King asked Vida.

"Let me handle that. I have an idea that might work," Colton answered for her.

"I'll leave that in your hands then. Good luck, Vida." King walked towards the door. "I need to get back to the club; I have to find someone to debug it tomorrow. When I find out who placed them in the first place, they are going to be fucked up," he stated ruthlessly.

"King, they couldn't find anything to get you for, could they?" Vida would feel terrible if King ended up in prison when he had offered to help. Vida didn't know how many of his activities were illegal, yet she was sure that he didn't always stay within the limits of the law.

"Don't worry about it, Vida. They have bigger fish to fry besides me." Vida wasn't so sure, however she had to let it go. King wasn't about to discuss his business with her, now or ever. Vida didn't know if anyone knew the complexities of King's business other than the man himself.

Colton locked the door behind King, glancing at his watch. "You need to start getting ready."

"All right." She gathered her clothes, trying not to be upset that King had looked more upset about her having to strip again than Colton had. He had claimed to care about her, yet he didn't seem the least perturbed about how she would be giving a private lap dance later that night.

Vida showered, making sure she shaved and moisturized her skin with the expensive smelling lotion that Sherri had told her drove the men crazy. Vida thought it was a little heady, but Sherri said that men found it sensual. Her boyfriend always provided her insights into a male's point-of-view and she had passed on the information to Vida.

Blowing out her hair until it lay straight and silky against her back, Vida dressed in a thick pair of sweats and a long sleeved t-shirt as the night would be cool on the back of Colton's bike. Deciding to wear the red outfit for the last time, she packed her bag and left the bathroom.

The living room and kitchen were empty. Fixing herself some soup, she heard Colton go into the shower. Pouring the hot soup into bowls and making a couple of fresh salads she sat down just as Colton came into the room, wearing a black t-shirt and jeans. Vida spooned some of her soup into her suddenly dry mouth. It wasn't fair that he was so sexy without the least effort. He had grown a small goatee and it only made him appear more like a bad boy biker, especially since the t-shirt was short sleeved and showed off his tats.

He sat down at the table and began eating, seeming as preoccupied as she did. Vida couldn't help wondering if he was regretting his divorce now that it was final. Not liking the feeling in her stomach when she discovered that she cared that he might regret his decision.

"Feeling nervous?" Vida smoothed out her expression at Colton's question.

"Not really. It's not like it's my first time." Vida blushed when she realized her choice of words.

Colton tried to smother his laughter. "Was it bad?"

Vida shuddered, remembering. "It was a joke. I'm surprised the men didn't ask for their cover charge back."

"It couldn't have been that bad."

"It took my dance, and two other women's turns on the stage to just get my top off. It was a nightmare. When it was over, I cried for two hours straight. You don't even want to know about my first lap dance. King did have to refund the man his money for that one."

This time Colton couldn't hold back his laughter. Rising to his feet, he took their dirty dishes to the sink.

Vida stood up, going to get her bag, but Colton forestalled her by taking her hand. "I'm not happy letting you do this, but I know you feel that you need to do this for Sawyer and the other women. No more after tonight, though," Colton forewarned her.

"Maybe the club won't be busy tonight." Vida hoped she was right.

"It's Friday, and all the horny men with no dates who want something to jerk of to will be there," he said sarcastically.

"Gee, thanks, I'll have that picture in my head now while I'm dancing."

"You better not be thinking of any of them fuckwads jerking off. I'll be there. Pretend it's just me you're dancing for."

"I don't think that will make it any easier," Vida said under her breath, not wanting to confess his presence would make her even more nervous.

"What?" Colton asked with a smile.

His arrogant attitude reminded her of the addition to her tattoo. "Why did you put your initials in my tattoo?"

Colton lost his smile becoming serious. "Because when

other men look at you, both of us will know who you really belong to, Vida."

"I don't belong to you," she protested.

"Baby, when you're on that stage tonight and I want to kill one of those motherfuckers staring at you, the only thing holding me back will be when I see my mark on you."

"Oh." Vida stared at his composed expression, sensing the lethal intent buried just below the surface.

"We done?" Vida nodded her head. "Let's go." She followed Colton out the door, dreading the next few hours.

It was going to be hard to go back on that stage when she had been so overjoyed that she was free from the humiliating experience. The lap dance she looked at with even more trepidation of having to be so close to Briggs. She really hated him and knew if he thought he could get away with it, he would take her, with or without her consent.

When they finally got into the club, it was immediately evident that Colton had been right. The club was extremely busy.

With a nudge to her back, Colton left her to go into the dressing room. Sherri was there, giving her a tight hug at her sudden appearance.

"I've been worried about you, kid. You doing okay?" she asked.

"I'm fine, Sherri," Vida assured the kindhearted woman who had taught her how to shed her clothes, not in the least jealous of Vida's popularity.

"You can go on before me if you want. They won't be as drunk. You're scheduled three spots after me. By then, they'll be so drunk the men will be trying to jump the stage," she offered.

Vida started to refuse.

"I don't mind. I'm used to them trying to get a piece of me," Sherri joked.

"Are you sure?"

"Positive. Besides, they tip better when they're drunk." She rubbed her hands together.

Vida smiled at her antics as she dressed in her outfit, putting on her stage make-up. Deciding not to tease her hair into a wild mess, she left it straight and then put on her red lipstick as the final touch. She stepped back from the mirror and looked at her changed appearance. No longer the college student, but a seductive woman with one goal; to see how much money she could tempt out of the men in a ten-minute set.

"You look hot tonight." Sherri's experienced eyes ran over Vida's body, taking in her new tattoo and the little bit of weight she had gained over the last week. "Something about you is different. That sexy ex-convict teaching you a thing or two?"

"No!" Vida evaded her question as she passed Sherri going into the restroom. There was nothing worse than a full bladder when you were shaking your boobs and ass at a roomful of men.

"Can he show me a thing or two?"

"No!" Vida yelled through the closed door.

"Damn."

Chapter Sixteen

Colton took a seat at a back table, facing the stage. A vibrant redhead was currently on the stage, shaking her tail for the front row, giving an incentive to place their money on her body. He ordered a beer when the waitress came to his table.

Colton's brow lifted when King joined him, taking a seat across from him.

"I didn't think you ever sat anywhere except your booth?"

"I can be flexible, especially when they have my booth bugged." Colton just bet King wasn't happy with that piece of information. He paid dearly for information from his contacts on the force, someone must be wising up to be able to bug King and him not know about it beforehand.

The redhead's music ended and Vida's began. Colton tensed in his seat when she came strutting out as if she owned the stage.

King smiled. "She's come a long way since her first night."

"So I've heard," Colton answered, not taking his eyes

off her as she twirled around the pole with one leg, her dark hair flying silkily around her.

"I bet you have. Several of the Predators became regulars on her nights. I don't see any of them here tonight. That's interesting," King said thoughtfully, staring at Colton.

"They're not here because I told them I would beat the shit out of them if they showed up," Colton said grimly as he watched Vida moving away from the pole, dancing suggestively in front of several men on the side of the stage before working her way over to the other side. She never glanced back towards the table that Colton sat at with King.

"That wasn't very friendly." King's amusement drew his attention briefly from Vida.

"There are a few questions I need answered, King."

All amusement at Colton's predicament ended when he saw that Colton was serious.

"What do you want to know?"

"I find it very interesting that Vida, from a neighborhood that's high in crime and has more punks trying to score pussy then any I know of in America, is a virgin who has managed to escape their attention."

King's face became an impassive mask. "Are you asking me why Vida is still a virgin? How would I know?"

"Because my brothers and I did a little digging, and I'm a little interested in what I found out."

"Exactly what did you find out?" King asked, his jaw tightening.

"That you put out the word for the punks and other unsavory elements to stay away or they would deal with you," Colton answered.

King shrugged. "I did that for Goldie."

"I don't think so. This order went out when she was just a kid, and it covered Sawyer. Seems this is what led Digger to them. He was searching for a way to get to you. How would going after them get to you?"

"If that is why Digger went after them, then that was his mistake. I have no emotional or physical connection to either Vida or Sawyer." King looked Colton straight in the eye.

Colton looked back at King. He had known him for years, ever since his stepdad had started bringing him in the strip club with the Predators. They had struck up a friendship over the years.

The man was lying, he could tell. What worried Colton was that King was an expert at lying, so if he could tell, his enemies could also, which placed Vida and Sawyer in danger.

The music changed. Colton looked toward the stage to see Vida taking off her red corset. Her pert breasts shone under the lights of the stage. Colton wanted to get up from the stage and punch a few of the men in the front row, but restrained himself this time.

Colton looked up into Vida's face, seeing her eyes were on him. They were full of humiliation. She was embarrassed she was doing it. Now, it was even worse because he was watching her. Colton let heat flow from his eyes, giving her a smile that let her know how pretty and fine he thought she was. He leaned across the table so that the lighting could catch his expression and let all the lust he had been holding back show in his face.

He noticed she had a small stumble before she managed to catch herself. Colton promised himself that one day, not too long from now, she would be standing in his bedroom, giving him the same exact performance, and he was going to throw her down on the bed and fuck her until she couldn't walk.

Vida turned red and Colton gave her a satisfied smile. She walked forward when the music changed again, getting close to the men in the front row, letting them slip bills into the string around her waist. One bastard trailed his fingers close to her pussy. Colton started to get up, but King's hand on his arm brought him back down in his seat as King motioned to Henry to escort the overzealous man out of the club.

After several minutes, Vida went to the stage, giving the men their last show of her ass.

"If she bends down and waves at them from between her legs, I am going to turn her ass bright red to match her outfit when I get her home," Colton threatened.

The words were no sooner out of his mouth than Vida did that exact move. Colton's jaw tightened.

"I don't think she heard you," King said with amusement.

"She's never going back on that stage again. I don't care how many women's lives she's trying to save."

"I agree."

Both men watched as Briggs ordered another whiskey.

"I hope you're giving him the good stuff." Colton eyed the liquor in Brigg's glass.

"What he's drinking is almost pure alcohol. Vida will be heading upstairs after she gets redressed and takes a fifteen minute break." King started to get out of his seat.

"King, what's the connection between you and the girls?" Colton tried one more time.

King opened his mouth then closed it sharply. "There isn't one, Colton." He moved away from the table, but not before he gave Colton a warning look to leave it alone. Aware they didn't know which areas of the club were bugged, Colton didn't go after him to find out what he needed to know to keep Vida safe.

Instead, Colton sat at his table and continued nursing his beer. Not long after, Briggs managed to stumble up the steps after he finished several whiskeys. Colton waited until he saw Vida climb the discreet stairway before he started after her.

As he was going up the stairs, he noticed several of the Predators entering the door, taking front row seats. He should have known Max wasn't going to miss Sherri's show.

He entered the VIP room to see Vida already being bought a drink from one of King's private customers that had watched her performance from the room. A huge, plate glass window provided a view of the stage, but anyone outside simply saw smoky glass.

Vida didn't pay him any attention when he entered the room and took a seat in the corner on an expensive couch. King had spared no expense in decorating the private room.

Two of the shot girls came to his table. Colton ordered another beer and told them to leave him alone.

"Not interested?" one of the shot girls asked. She was shorter than the taller, curvier one. Colton would have taken a shot from her once upon a time, before Vida.

Colton shrugged. "No thanks." He didn't take his eyes off Vida.

"If you change your mind, let me know." The blond, short one bent over to whisper, "I get off at three. I'll let you take shots all night for free".

"No, thanks. I'm with someone." Colton nodded his head towards Vida.

She gave a smile. "Lucky girl." The shorter one went back to the bar for his beer.

The taller one bent over the table, giving him a view of her tits.

"My name's Krystal. I can keep my mouth shut if you change your mind later." She nodded her head to Vida. "She's a sweet kid, but I can suck your dick like you've never had it done before."

The other woman returned, setting down the beer. They started to move away, but Colton's words halted them both.

"I won't be needing anything else tonight." His cold voice left no doubt that he didn't want to be bothered again.

Taking a drink of his beer, he noticed Briggs move to stand beside Vida, who was already talking to another customer. She played it cool, gradually changing focus from one man to the other, seeming reluctant at first then more willing to talk to him.

Colton saw Briggs's hand wander over Vida's ass several times while she kept moving out of his reach, shaking her head no. Briggs picked up his drink, downing it in one swallow.

Vida moved towards the room where she would give the lap dance with Briggs, who followed after her like he was on a leash. Colton wanted to beat the man until he had several broken bones; instead, he had to watch.

Colton moved to where he could watch her performance continue through the glass. He was only going to give Vida enough time to get what information she needed then he was going to shut her act down. After that, he knew exactly how she was going to spend the rest of her night.

* * *

Vida closed the door to the private room, feeling Colton's eyes on her back, certain he was even now moving towards the window to watch her from the window. Briggs sat down in the chair. He was definitely drunk, and probably was a little high from the glazed look in his eyes. Both conditions she hoped would help her get the information she needed without her having to spend much time in his vicinity.

"Come here, Trouble," Briggs crooned to her.

Vida turned away in disgust, hitting the button by the door that would fill the room with music. Putting the best sway into her hips she could manage, she neared his chair and leaned over him, giving him an eyeful of her cleavage.

"Come closer."

Vida knew he wanted her on top of him.

"I'm mad at you, Briggs. I thought we had something special going on, and you didn't even try to help me with Digger. You were going to let him have me when you knew how bad I wanted you," she said in a fake, stupid

150

voice that she had heard the other women use hundreds of times.

"You seemed close to Colton. I didn't seem too important to you, Vida."

"I was mad at you. I didn't want Digger. You were going to take me to his bedroom."

"I wasn't going to leave you alone with him. Digger doesn't mind sharing," he confirmed that he would have raped her that night.

"He doesn't?" she asked, trying to stay on track.

"No, I would have made sure he treated you good. You would have had a time you would have never forgotten." Vida just bet she wouldn't have forgotten; being raped by two men at the same time tended to have that effect. He sickened her by believing she would have enjoyed the experience.

Vida moved closer, straddling his lap without giving him her weight. Wiggling and twisting above his lap, she forced herself to rub her breasts against his chest, heightening his desire.

"I don't understand why he took me in the first place," Vida probed.

"He hates King."

Vida almost stopped her lap dance.

"What do I have to do with King?"

"Both you and Sawyer are under King's protection. Everyone knows that the only one King ever extended that protection to was his sister, and he dismembered the man that was responsible for her death. Every shithead in town was afraid to mess with you and Sawyer. Digger wasn't, he hates King, wanted to make King get mad enough to make a mistake and take him out."

Vida let a tiny amount of her weight drop down on his crotch. "Sawyer's disappearance and mine both show that we didn't mean anything to him. He ignored the situation until I asked for his help, and he hasn't gone crazy trying to go after Digger."

Briggs grabbed her hips, trying to force more of her weight down on him. Vida could see he was practically grinding his teeth in his desire for more of her.

"Digger was surprised. When he took Sawyer, he messed her up trying to find out her connection to King, but she didn't know anything. The only thing she came up with was she remembered an incident when you were kids and King had been going to see someone in the building you lived in. He had stopped to talk to you girls, but she didn't remember what it was about. I'm not surprised Digger had her so high she could barely remember her name."

If Vida had a gun, she would shoot him and not mind spending the rest of her life in prison. She was sure Colton and Sawyer would visit her. Vida didn't remember King ever talking to them when they were little, however Sawyer was older than her and would have a better memory.

Vida knew a way to get even and spend no time in prison herself. Determined, she let more of her weight fall against his crotch, grinding herself against him, trying not to shudder in disgust.

"I don't know why Digger cares about King. He is obviously the smarter one. I was looking forward to partying with him," Vida lied, rising up from Briggs's lap as he tried to arch his hips against her.

"He is; no one can touch him. He has women all over the place, even movie stars and musicians call for him to provide him with entertainment," Briggs bragged drunkenly.

"Movie stars? Musicians? Do you mean Rock stars?" Vida asked in an awestruck voice.

"We charge a fucking fortune to provide them with a fuck that won't go running to the tabloids to sell their story."

"How can you stop them from talking?" Vida questioned.

"Digger sells them with the others when the star is

done with her. The men don't care; they just want their own personal little sex slave. They disappear, never to be heard from again. Their buyers make sure of that." Vida shivered at Briggs's smug face.

The idiot was bragging, not caring that he was telling her that Digger had the same fate in store for her if Colton hadn't rescued her. They were freaking psycho's. Suddenly, Vida remembered something from her introductory psychology course she had to take in college. Psychopaths couldn't understand or care that their victims suffered pain, but pain to them was excruciating.

"But how can he keep all these women and no one knows? I imagine it has to be pretty isolated where no one can see or hear anything." Vida tried to gather more information, not sure how much longer she could tolerate being this close to the monster.

Briggs almost came to his senses, his ingrained fear of Digger fighting the haze that alcohol and drugs had enveloped his senses in. Vida, seeing reason momentarily return to his beady little eyes, began rubbing herself faster against him. Leaning forward, her fingertips traced the sensitive veins in his neck that were standing out.

When he didn't answer, Vida's hips rose an inch from his and she pulled her breasts away, removing her hands from underneath his shirt.

"Don't stop," Briggs begged. "He has several locations. It's like a fucking bus station; he moves them from one location to the next. They all are isolated houses, except for the one here in town."

He continued, his hands going to her ass, "It's right under the police's fucking nose. The recording studio in town that advertises all over the country as having the best rates and sound techs available. The whole building is soundproof. Digger gets fresh stock in all the time, and he doesn't even have to leave the building. The upper floors are legit, but the basement is used to train the sweet things until Digger moves them out. By the time we get done with them, they walk right out the front door and into the waiting car. I told you Digger is a fucking genius," Briggs gloated, wanting her to admire the brilliance of Digger's plan.

Digger might be a genius, but his hired help was a moron. Vida, with the information she needed and unable to stomach one more second near him without throwing up, was relieved when she heard the door open and Colton come in the room.

"What the fuck is going on in here?" he yelled.

Fear flooded Briggs's face as Colton slammed the door back against the wall.

"Colton, I told you I had to work tonight." Vida gave a fake squeak of fear as Colton placed his hands around her waist and lifted her off Briggs.

Viciously, Vida made sure that her thick, high-heeled stripper shoe snapped up and kicked Briggs in the balls as hard as she could manage. His scream of pain could be heard, Vida was sure, downstairs. That thought gave her some satisfaction.

"You fucking bitch!" Briggs held himself, crying like a baby.

"Watch your mouth," Colton growled.

"What's going on in here?" Henry's amused voice had everyone looking at the huge man.

"The fucking…" Colton's furious gaze had Briggs changing his mind about his choice of words. "Vida kicked me in the balls."

"It was an accident, Henry. Colton pulled me off of him. I didn't mean to. I wouldn't hurt you deliberately; you're one of my favorites." She batted her false eyelashes at him.

"I'm sure King will refund your money, Briggs. We do want our customers completely satisfied. Ashley will give you a dance on the house also. Does that sound reasonable, Briggs?"

Mollified, Briggs sat back, rubbing his abused crotch.

"Let's go, Vida and Colton. Vida, King will have to let you go because of this second complaint from a customer. We can't have them hurt because a dancer's boyfriend becomes jealous." Briggs's head swelled even further at the thought that Colton could possibly be jealous of him.

As Vida and Colton left the room, she gave a sigh of relief when she heard the door close behind them. Colton's arm came around her shoulders.

"Did you get what you needed?" Colton asked.

"I think so. Colton, they're really sick and have to be stopped." Vida told him with resolution.

"I know, baby. That was the only reason I could let you back on that stage again, much less let that motherfucker touch you."

"You better get out of here," Henry said, motioning for Ashley, who slid past them with a bottle of King's best whiskey in her hand.

Vida felt sorry for the pretty blond who would have to let Briggs touch her so that he would forget the fountain of information he had provided them with.

Interpreting her look, Colton sought to reassure her. "By the time he's a fourth of the way through that bottle, he won't remember his own name, and she can leave."

Vida nodded.

Colton and Vida went to the dressing room to retrieve her bag. She didn't want to take the time to change, needing to go home and get further away from the pollution still upstairs. Understanding, Sherri let her borrow a long raincoat, which she used in her act sometimes, that covered her completely. Vida put it on and, giving Sherri a quick hug of thanks, left to find Colton waiting outside the door.

Colton waved to King as they left, who returned it with a grim nod as he talked on the phone. Vida could tell from his expression he was giving the other person on the line hell. By morning, Vida was sure every bug in his club would disappear.

"Should I call Seth?" she questioned Colton.

"That's who King is talking to. I gave him the number you gave me," Colton informed her.

A large man rose from a table they were passing close to the stage. Vida's stomach plunged when she recognized the man from the farmers' market that Colton had fought. Glancing quickly at the table, she became even more upset when she recognized the two others among the nine men seated.

"Well, looks like we found Trouble after all, boys." He snickered. "Charlie recognized you when you were on the stage," he said, giving her an insolent look. "You being with her, now that's just icing on the cake."

"Move." Colton took Vida's arm, moving her to his side, further away from the group of men.

"Make me, asshole. I don't think you'll be able to take us all on. When we're done with you, we're going to show that slut how a real man fucks." He laughed with the others following his lead. They started whistling and name calling Vida.

Vida wanted to get out of the club before a fight broke out. She looked around the room for Henry before she realized he must still be upstairs keeping an eye on Briggs.

"Need any help, Colton?" a cold voice had her turning sideways to see Ice, Max and several of the other Predators getting up from their chairs at the front of the stage. She noticed the one with the scar stood before casually striding out the front door.

"I got it covered, Ice. These fuckwads couldn't fight their way out of a whore's pussy."

"Dave, you gonna take that shit?" A loudmouth sitting at the back of the group hadn't noticed the arrival of the Predators.

"No, I don't think I am." Dave seemed bolstered from Colton's friends' presence, which just proved how stupid he was. "I'm going to kick your ass."

Colton took a step toward Dave and Vida pulled him

back.

"Colton, remember you're on parole. If you get caught, you could get your parole revoked. He's not worth it. Let's go home," she pleaded. The thought of him getting thrown back in prison, this time because of her, wasn't something she would be able to handle. "Please, Colton, ignore him."

"Shut-up, and take your tits and ass over there." Dave pointed to the stage where Sherri stood frozen in place, ignoring her music. "Me and my friends will take care of you when we finish."

Max moved closer. "Fuck this shit. I'm not on parole." His fist struck out, sending Dave hurtling onto the table. Bottles of beer went flying as the men stood up, each becoming ready to fight.

"Gentleman, I want you to leave." King's sudden appearance with several of his bouncers as the fight started to get out of control had the men pausing briefly.

Dave and his friends came to their senses when faced by even more opposition.

"We're leaving," he grumbled as they began to head to the door followed by the bouncers.

"Thanks, King," Vida said, relieved.

"No thanks needed, Vida. I wasn't going to have to pay for the damages to my club. Those fuckers don't look like they could afford one of my chairs."

Vida had to agree. "Can we go now?" she asked Colton.

"Go out back. I'll send Henry to give you a ride in my car," King ordered.

"Why not take his bike?"

"Because I think the police will be called any minute." Vida didn't understand what King meant until she realized the Predators had also gone outside. The bouncer's hadn't returned, either.

"Oh."

"Let's go," Colton said with a satisfied smile.

Henry was waiting for them at the back door. He had come down the back stairway. As he saw their approach, he opened the back door, looking outside before holding the door open for them.

Colton and Vida slid into the back seat as Henry started the car, pulling out of the alley onto the main road. Henry turned the car towards the direction of Colton's apartment.

When they passed the front of the King's club, Henry slowed the car as they stared at the huge fight in the parking lot. Ice and Max were beating on Dave. Vida almost felt sorry for him until she remembered he could have led to Colton being back in prison.

Vida's eyes glanced off one fighting pair before they went back in shock. The biker with the scar who had left the club had the heckler down on the ground. Vida turned, burying her head in Colton's shoulder at the viciousness of his attack on the man.

Thank God, King had stopped them from going outside. There was no way the cops wouldn't be locking up several of the men fighting while sending others to the local hospital.

During the ride back to the apartment Vida's thoughts returned to those poor women who didn't have their freedom. They had no choice in who took their bodies, captive and broken, and bent them to someone else's will.

Vida rolled down her window so the wind could hit her face, missing Colton's motorcycle. She leaned closer to Colton, needing his strength as she reminded herself Sawyer was still one of those women.

Chapter Seventeen

Vida felt Colton's eyes searching her face as they got out of the car. His arm went around her shoulders while they walked up the stairs side by side. When she turned back towards the car, Henry waved as he drove silently out of the parking lot.

After closing the door behind them, Colton went to the kitchen.

"Sit down. I'm going to fix you a drink." Vida kept on the coat as she sat on the couch and buried her face in her hands.

"Here" Colton handed her a glass with whiskey and ice. Vida made a face at the strong taste. "Drink it; it'll help you sleep." Vida sipped her drink as Colton sat down next to her.

"That was the worst thing I've ever had to do in my life." Vida shuddered. "He was telling me how and where they put those women, and I just wanted to vomit, but I had to pretend I wanted him."

"Vida, maybe now they can shut down the bastards and put them away," he said grimly.

"God, Colton, I hope so. I keep thinking of Sawyer;

how scared she must be, who has her, if he..."

"Don't think about it tonight, Vida. It's bad enough without you thinking about it constantly."

Vida stared at her hands, realizing that she still had on her red gloves. Staring blankly, all she could see was Sawyers face staring back at her.

"She's so shy, Colton. Her mom was really overprotective because of Sawyer's father getting killed so young. She was terrified something would happen to Sawyer. After the fire, she was even worse. She never let Sawyer have fun, or go places with her friends. When her mom died, Sawyer started going out more, but she was so shy. She just didn't fit in. Gradually, she stopped trying to go out very much. That was why I was so happy that she was excited about going out with this new guy she'd met. We tell each other everything. She hadn't had sex before. If they raped her..." Vida began crying.

"Vida, please stop, baby."

Colton pulled her onto his lap until she was facing him. "Let's get all this out of your mind for a few hours at least."

Unbuttoning the coat, he pulled it off. Vida sat facing him with her knees on the couch next to his hips. It was the same position that she had been in an hour ago with Briggs except now the feeling inside of her wasn't disgust; it was a low hum of pleasure that was growing inside of her belly.

"Colton, I need to go to bed. I'm tired."

"If you go to sleep now, you'll be tossing and turning all night. Let's neck awhile then you'll sleep like a baby."

"I don't like it when you call me, baby." Vida stood up on her knees over him, preparing to go shower.

Colton's hands went to her hips, clenching them in a tight grip.

"Why? When I touch you, I feel how fucking soft your skin is and it reminds me how I plan to take such good care of you." The suggestive look on his face left little doubt in her mind exactly how he planned to take care of her.

"Red is definitely your color, but I prefer that black scrap of material you had on the first time I saw you on stage. I could see your little pink nipples and that tiny piece of material over your pussy and all I could think about was how hard and fast I could fuck you before I came."

Vida started to tremble as his hand reached up and began unbuttoning her corset top. She reached out to grab his wrists, but she didn't exert any strength to stop him from exposing her breasts. Colton leaned forward and took her nipple into his mouth, biting down gently until she leaned closer, giving in to his silent demand. His teeth released her and his tongue gently began to lave the hardened tip.

She had clung to her virginity as a way to protect herself from getting hurt, yet Colton had her body and mind in turmoil. The problem was, she had fallen in love with a man that protected his wife enough to go to prison for her, who was loyal despite the ultimate betrayal. Colton would never be a Prince Charming, but he could be her knight in shining armor, if she took the leap.

Vida's head fell back and her body arched towards his. Colton's hands fell to her stocking covered thighs, sliding upwards until they reached the naked flesh of her upper thighs, gliding to her mound covered by the tiny red panties.

His fingers slid underneath, expertly finding the tiny bundle of hidden nerves. He stroked the delicate flesh until she thought she would scream. Still unsatisfied from the last time he had played with her, it didn't take long before Vida was squirming on his lap.

One long finger entered her tight sheath and she couldn't help the slight wince of pain. Colton's thumb rubbed harder against her clit, easing the finger out before moving it steadily back inside of her, creating a rhythmic stroking that had her leaning forward to kiss him, pushing her tongue into his mouth. Colton chuckled at her attempt of aggressiveness, letting her have her way with his mouth while he added another finger to the one steadily pumping inside of her.

Vida felt her hips bucking against his fingers until he was steadily fucking their long length inside her.

"Baby, you're little pussy is going to have some trouble taking my cock at first, but I have to get myself under control first. If I fuck you now, I might hurt you." Vida couldn't make sense of his words. The fire burning her up from inside was demanding she move faster and faster, trying to get release.

Colton lifted her off his lap, standing her on her feet. She wobbled a little, still wearing her plastic, high-heeled stripper shoes.

Colton looked down, staring at her feet and tracing her body with his gaze as he rose. Seeing her wobble, he lifted her up into his arms and carried her into his bedroom.

Vida heard the door snap closed, remembering how many times she'd heard that sound the last month when he had brought other women in to share his bed. She tried to jerk out of his arms, but Colton held her firm.

Laying her gently on the end of the bed, he pulled her panties off, causing her to fall backwards. He went to his knees beside the bed, spreading her thighs until she was opened and his mouth landed on her pussy with his tongue thrusting deep within her. His piercing sliding across the tender flesh of her opening had Vida's hips lurching off the bed, driving his tongue deeper within her.

Restraint and reason had gone in a heartbeat. Vida couldn't believe the passion rising from her, or the needy cries escaping her mouth.

"Oh please, Colton. Harder, suck me harder," Vida pleaded, writhing under his merciless teasing. Each time he felt her about to come he pulled away, not giving her the least touch to bring her over into ecstasy.

Colton rose to his feet then, pulling off his black t-shirt

and shoes before sitting on the side of the bed and removing his jeans. His hard cock rose from his lap, startling Vida with its large size.

Colton buried his hand in Vida's dark hair. "Come here." He scooted back to lean against the headboard and Vida followed him, directed by the hand in her hair, beginning to feel apprehensive. She was sure she had passed the no-going-back stage, yet she was beginning to doubt she wanted to go any further.

"We'll stop whenever you want," Colton assured her. Vida relaxed somehow, believing that he would stop whenever she wanted him to, she was, however, unsure if she really wanted to stop; that was a question her mind skirted. She felt a sense of power at the realization that she had big, bad Colton waiting for her to decide just how far she would let him go.

Vida started to kick her shoes off.

"Leave them on. I want to watch you suck my dick with those shoes on." His hand in her hair directed her mouth to hover directly over his cock.

Vida couldn't believe how badly she wanted to taste him. She had never been tempted before, but the idea of him in her mouth had her pussy clenching in need.

Her mouth opened and Colton surged between her parted lips. His legs opened wider as he pulled her head closer to his pelvis.

Vida almost choked on his length, and he immediately used her hair to pull her off him so that she could breath.

Vida heard his panting breath. Feminine satisfaction giving her confidence when his body broke out in a sheen of sweat. Their mouths met in a kiss that showed her heightened lust. She used her tongue to search his mouth before teasing the sensuous curve of his bottom lip, gently licking his piercing. Colton stiffened, his body hardening, as he held his strength in check. The power Vida felt over him was driving her own passion higher.

He gradually tugged her back down onto his hard cock.

This time Vida wasn't as apprehensive, getting used to the demanding hand at the back of her head. Her own hand reached out to squeeze his cock halfway down so that she wouldn't take too much of him. Setting up a rhythm that had his hips pumping steadily, Vida loved the feeling of having him under her control.

"I'm never going to forget how you looked the first time you took my cock, Vida. You're so fucking unbelievably sexy with that outfit on; those shoes and your little mouth sucking on my cock like you can't get enough. One night I'm going to video you sucking my dick then let you watch it while I fuck you."

Vida shook her head. Colton laughed. "You think I can't keep something like that safe from other's eyes? Baby, I would never let anyone see you like this, wanting me with your pink nipples and wet pussy. But it will make you so hot you'll beg me to fuck you."

Vida didn't doubt him; the way he was talking to her was having the same effect with merely his words placing the images in her mind. Vida felt him bucking harder against her mouth, his body stiffening and then he jerked away from her. Colton got up from the bed, leaving Vida gasping at his departure, wondering where he had gone. The water in the bathroom running answered her question. Vida lay still when Colton came back, pulling her from the bed before he pushed her down on the side of the bed, taking off one high heel then the other. Picking her up, he tossed her onto the middle of the bed, lying down beside her before he reached over and turned out the light.

"Colton, I don't understand." Vida lay confused, her body still in need.

"Vida, I'm trying to show you that I can be the man you need me to be, but if you keep flashing that pussy up at me, I won't give a damn that you haven't made up your mind yet about us and I will fuck you until you have to crawl off that mattress in the morning.

"Get some sleep. Tomorrow is my turn to open the

shop. I'm not going to take your virginity when you're still upset about Briggs and Sawyer. We have plenty of time." He pulled her towards him until she lay against his chest with her head on his shoulder.

Vida forced herself to lay still, but her body didn't listen. She was restless with the need he had woken then left unsatisfied not once but twice now. Vida was beginning to resent not only him, but also her virginity. Sure, if she was more experienced, she would be feeling him inside of her right now. Pushing those thoughts from her mind, his firm hand stroking her back finally eased enough tension that she was able to fall asleep.

* * *

Vida recognized the woman coming in the shop from the strip club. She worked in the VIP room, and was very popular with the men there, which was how she had managed to work herself up from performing on the stage to just having to perform for the richer patrons who liked to hang out at the club in the autonomy the VIP room provided.

"Hi, Krystal," Vida greeted her unhappily, betting herself a fictitious million dollars just why she was there.

"Hey, Vida." The woman came forward to lean against the counter. "I want a new tattoo."

"All right. Where do you want the tattoo?" Vida questioned.

Krystal gave her a smile and a wink. "On the upper check of my butt."

Vida stared down at the appointment book, knowing who was up for the next walk-in, knowing she would be unable to slide it past either Colton or Tessa without each aware of what she was doing. She was stuck.

"Have a seat. Colton will be with you in about twenty minutes."

"Thanks, Vida."

Vida watched out of the corner of her eye as Krystal reapplied her lipstick and then crossed her legs, which were exposed to perfection by her little blue jean skirt. Vida felt dowdy in her blue jeans and t-shirt. She hadn't had time to do laundry and had grabbed one out of Colton's drawers. It hung from her body.

Vida unconsciously began chewing on the pencil she used to schedule appointments instead of paying attention to the attractive woman waiting for Colton to appear.

Colton walked into the room, talking to his client about the aftercare of his new tattoo. Then, after the customer left, he walked behind the counter, looking at his next appointment. He gave her a mischievous grin when he looked across the room and Krystal rose to her feet.

"Krystal?"

"Yes." The woman breathed, attempting seduction in her response. Vida's teeth clenched.

"What tattoo are you wanting?" Vida had to kick herself when she saw Colton's amusement; the asshole knew she was jealous.

"I want a rose on the upper part of my butt." She turned around, giving him an eyeful of her pert ass, her hand pointing to exactly where she wanted the tattoo placed. "Can you do that?"

"I sure can. Let's go to my room." Colton gave Vida a wicked grin before escorting Krystal from the room, passing Tessa and her client as they left.

Vida sat tensely, lost in thought, not even paying attention when Tessa came to stand next to her after her client departed. Vida could tell from her expression she wanted to say something sarcastic, yet she managed to restrain herself, merely giving Vida a caustic order.

"Call me when my client arrives."

"All right."

Vida tried to occupy herself, filling out several job applications in states Sawyer and she had dreamed of visiting after Vida graduated. Out of curiosity, Vida searched the help wanted nearby Colton's shop. She was surprised that there were two positions for computer programmers that would be opening in the next month.

Impulsively, Vida filled out the applications online, pressing the submit button just as Colton and Krystal walked into the lobby. She was giving him a flirtatious smile as she asked if he would come over tonight and rub the lotion on her because she didn't know how she could possible reach it.

The pencil in her hand snapped and she closed her computer. Not waiting to hear his response, Vida rose to her feet.

"I'm going to go across the street and get a cup of coffee. I'll be back in five minutes," Vida snapped.

"Wait a minute, Vida." Catching her hand when she would have stormed by them, he pulled her to his side.

"Sorry, Krystal. Vida and I are busy tonight. I'm sure you'll manage just fine."

Krystal didn't try to hide her disappointment, looking Vida over in her oversized clothes. "Call me if anything changes, Colton." Leaving a furious Vida and an amused Colton, the woman left before Vida could smack her silly.

"Well, if that isn't too sweet," Tessa said mockingly. "You both look so cute together."

"Tessa, don't start." Vida heard the warning in Colton's voice. As usual, Tessa ignored it, walking forward with a look in her eyes that had chills of warning running down Vida's back.

"My client just called, cancelling his appointment, so I'm done for the day," Tessa told Colton.

"That's fine. See you Monday." Colton tried to shut her down, but Vida could tell the woman was out for blood.

"Thanks, it works out for me since I'm going out with Roni tonight. You remember her, don't you, Colton?" Vida felt Colton stiffen next to her.

"You and Vida should join us. The four of us can sit around and talk about how good you are at fucking, and you can sit back and glory in how much pussy that dick you're so proud of gets."

"Shut up, Tessa. Leave now." Colton made another attempt to head off the confrontation.

A cruel smile twisted her lips. "She knows you, too, Vida."

Vida racked her memory for a face for the unfamiliar name, coming up with a blank.

"When I mentioned your name, she said she knew your mother. Asked how you were doing. Seems like your mom and her were friends, even shared the stage together a few times, from what she tells me. They liked to party together too. Colton, don't you remember?

"Roni said that Goldie talked about Vida all the time. You even used to call Goldie to party with you when Roni had to work and she didn't. She told me about the good times you used to have together. You really should talk to her, Vida. It would be a real eye opener. Of course, you may not mind that the man you're fucking also fucked your mother, but it freaks me out."

"Get out, Tessa, and don't come back. You're finished here, forever. If you even try to come in the door, I'll call the cops and have you arrested. It would give you a taste of what I had for three years."

"Colton... you don't mean it." Tessa's face was suddenly as white as Vida's.

"Get the fuck out or I will throw you out." Colton's face was a mask of fury that was barely held in check. Tessa realized too late that she had finally cut the final thread with Colton. He was done with her.

Vida, through her own pain and horror, could plainly see that Colton never wanted Tessa near him again. When Tessa finally ran out the door, it left both Vida and Colton staring after her.

Vida tore her hand from Colton's grip, backing away from him. Going to the counter, she packed her computer into her backpack.

"Vida." Colton's soft voice drew her eyes to him. "Let me explain."

"Just answer one question for me."

Colton ran his fingers through his long hair and then crossed his arms across his chest. Vida could tell he was bracing himself for her question. "Go ahead."

"Is what she said the truth?"

"Yes and no." Anger flew through Vida's mind. Storming into her was the hurt that he had never told her. He had listened to her talk about her mother and never mentioned he was one of the men who had briefly used her. To think that he had touched her, that she had even wanted to have sex with him last night, humiliated and sickened her.

"You sick bastard!" Vida screamed at him. Jerking up her backpack, she ran for the front door, only to find it blocked with Colton standing in her path.

"Vida, listen to me. I'll tell you everything you want to know. Calm down."

"Don't tell me to calm down you... you... perv." Angered beyond reasoning, she swung her backpack with the computer in it, hitting him before he managed to jerk it from her hands.

She turned to run for the door, but his arm around her waist prevented her from going out the door. He lifted her off the floor as she struggled, her feet kicking back towards him, trying to gain her release. Colton reached out, locking the door and turning the open sign off before walking with her struggling body back to his room.

Shutting the door behind them, he let her go and then leaned back against the door, blocking any chance of escape she had.

Shaking her hair off her face and getting her breathing under control, Vida threw him a dirty look. "Let me out, Colton."

"Where do you plan on going?"

"I'm going to stay at King's place until Sawyer gets back next week. Then, I'm gone."

"You go back to King, you have to start stripping

again."

"That's better than staying with a pervert like you," Vida yelled at him.

"Don't call me that, it's not nice and it's not true. You know it's not. I could have fucked you anytime in the last week instead of letting you tease me until my balls are blue."

"How about you go fuck yourself?" Vida yelled.

"How about I fuck you instead?" he countered, becoming angry.

Vida looked around the room for something else to hit him with, however he was on her before she could find anything. He picked her up and tossed her onto the large couch against the wall, pinning her underneath his heavy weight. Vida tried to scratch at him with her nails and found both of her hands held in one of his above her head.

Vida continued to grapple against him until she wore herself out, lying limply underneath him. She turned her face to the side so she at least wouldn't have to look at him.

"Finished?" Colton's grim face stared down at her.

Vida didn't acknowledge him.

"Good. Now you're going to listen to me." Colton relaxed against her. His jean covered cock finding the notch of her thighs.

"I met your mother when I joined the Predators; she was seeing one of the brothers. When they broke up, she had made several friends, one of them was Roni. She was twenty, Vida, younger than you are now. I was sixteen, but I became involved with Roni on and off for the next couple of years. I never touched your mother. My mouth or hands were never in the vicinity of her body. I did mess around with Roni and several of the other women at the clubhouse, but not Goldie. We were never attracted to each other; we became friends and did party together a lot. It was some pretty hardcore partying, Vida, but I never had her, not once."

"Why didn't you tell me you knew my mother?" Vida whispered. The anger was gone, but the hurt remained.

"Because I liked your mom and I truthfully didn't want you asking me questions about her that I knew would hurt you if I gave you the truth."

"She was a slut, wasn't she?"

"No, honey, but she was constantly looking for a man. She didn't like being alone, Vida. She wanted a man to share her life with."

"She had me." Vida bit her lip to keep it from trembling.

"Baby, she loved you, never doubt that, but it just wasn't enough for her. She wasn't like you. You're strong, Vida. Strong enough to stand on that stage and bare your body and soul to save your friend. You put your disgust aside to assist in finding women who need help simply because you couldn't turn your back and walk away. There's no one else like you, Vida. Even your own mother, who was the sweetest woman I've ever met, can't compare to you."

He released her hands. Vida lowered them, circling his shoulders and then looking up into his eyes. She could tell he was telling the truth.

"I'm sorry I hit you with my computer and called you a perv," Vida apologized.

Colton grinned down at her. "Is that all you're sorry for?"

"Did I call you something else?" Vida tried to think of all the names she had called him out loud. He couldn't expect her to apologize for the ones that she had in her head when she hadn't voiced them.

"No, I'm talking about something else."

"What?" Vida asked suspiciously.

"My blue balls."

"Oh." A smile teased her lips. "Why should I have to apologize for that? You didn't tell me you were sorry for leaving me in the same shape," Vida informed him unwisely.

"You have blue balls?"

"No. You know what I mean." Blushing Vida buried her face in his shoulder.

"Oh, did I leave my baby hanging? Is that what you meant?"

Vida was glad he couldn't see her face, but she nodded her head against him.

"Well, I can't break my promise about taking good care of you, can I?"

"No," Vida mumbled, unable to believe she was urging him on.

Colton rose up to sit on his knees between her thighs, pulling his shirt up and off. Vida stared at his chest covered in various tattoos. Her mouth went dry when she saw a couple disappear beneath the band of his jeans. His hand tugged her shirt off before unsnapping the flimsy pink bra she had on underneath.

"There are my pretty girls." He leaned down, grazing each breast with a light kiss against their tip. Getting off the couch, he pulled his shoes and jeans off before pulling off Vida's.

She started to protest when he pulled off her underwear, but she didn't, knowing he would stop when she asked.

For the first time, Vida enjoyed showing her naked body, thrilled that Colton enjoyed seeing it displayed before him. His hardening cock showed how much he wanted her. When he would have lain back down on the couch with her, Vida rose to her knees. Before he could guess what her next move was, she surrounded the head of his cock with her mouth, sucking his length into her throat. This time, when Vida would have welcomed the roughness of the night before, he remained gentle, letting her have only the tip.

His finger went to her pussy, separating the cleft until

his fingers swirled in the moistness that seeing him naked had provided.

"Your little pussy is nice and wet, Vida. You like having me in your mouth, don't you?"

Vida nodded against him. It was the truth; something about taking him in her mouth, knowing he was at her mercy, made her want him. It was a strange and frightening thing to want that part of him. The thought of him wanting another woman like Krystal, Tammy or Tessa drove her on to prove to herself that she was all he would need to satisfy those desires she saw swirling in the depths of his eyes.

Vida was an innocent, however she had learnt one thing the last few weeks at King's; you control a man's cock, you control him.

"I don't even want to know what you're thinking right now. I have a feeling it's better if I never do," Colton said wryly.

"I was just thinking that I love the taste of you." Colton's eyes narrowed, not believing her for a second.

"You know what feels even better?"

"No, what?" Vida asked, trying to drive him crazy by swirling her tongue over the crest of his cock.

Colton pulled away from her to sit down on the couch, pulling her onto his lap, her knees on each side of his hips. His cock rubbed against her wet heat and Vida pressed down harder against him. The increased pressure almost sent her over the edge.

"You want me, baby?"

Vida wanted him so bad she ached. All the doubts she had disappeared and she knew exactly what she wanted. "I want you, Colton."

Colton lifted her by her hips until the tip of his cock brushed against her entrance. Her hands gripped his shoulders, balancing on her knees as he slowly brought her down on him. She felt him pushing to get inside of her and it made her want to slam herself down on his cock, but his tight grip on her hips kept her from moving.

"Coltonnn... please... fuck... me..." Vida tried to wiggle down further on him, but he gritted his teeth.

"I'm trying not to hurt you."

"It couldn't feel worse than this," Vida protested.

Ignoring her, he slid another small inch inside of her.

Vida wanted more. She leaned forward, taking his nipple in her mouth, biting down.

"Dammit, Vida." Colton's hips surged upward, tearing through her hymen in one hard thrust. Vida fell against his chest. "Did I hurt you?

"No," Vida lied.

"Don't lie to me, baby. I wanted to make this a beautiful experience for you. I meant to have you for the first time on a bed, not a couch," he said regretfully.

"You are making it beautiful, Colton," Vida whispered into his neck.

Colton's fingers went to the juncture of her thighs. Finding her clit, he stroked her until Vida gradually began moving on his cock, wincing slightly when he slid even deeper.

Colton's hands went behind his head. "Pretend you're giving me a lap dance."

"What?"

"Think of your favorite song then pretend you're giving me a lap dance."

Vida thought of her favorite song then gradually began moving on top of him. Teasing him with faint brushes of her breasts against his chest. She slowly moved her hips back and forth against him, instead of up and down. The friction against her brought her passion back with a vengeance.

"Oh." Vida stared at him with desire plain in her eyes.

Colton grinned back at her. "Feels good, doesn't it?"

"It's incredible." Vida let the music in her mind lead her body into taking over.

She quit thinking, grinding down on Colton, driving his

cock deep within her. She began moving faster as she increased the speed, feeling herself coming closer and closer. Every time she came down she ground herself against him, giving herself the stimulation she needed.

Colton leaned forward suddenly, his hips thrusting upwards as she came down hard on him. She clenched him, squeezing him tight as she came in a climax that had her rocking against him until he held her still, thrusting high inside of her. A series of jerks within her had her going over the edge into ecstasy again.

"Fuck," Vida said, her head falling forward. Exhausted, she lay against him.

Colton's body was shaking. Vida raised her head to find that he was silently laughing down at her.

"Are you laughing at me?" she asked in disbelief.

"Kind of."

"Why?" The last thing a woman wanted to hear was the man she just had sex with laughing.

"Baby, you're every man's fantasy. Not only do you fuck like you can't get enough of my dick, but you talk dirty. A man couldn't ask for more."

"A woman could," Vida responded.

"I couldn't give you more right now if someone put a gun to my head," Colton joked, pulling her forward until he softly kissed her lips. "Thank you."

Vida knew what he was thanking her for. "You're welcome."

"Feel like getting a tattoo?"

Vida thought at first he was joking, but she actually did. "Yes, I never want to forget tonight."

"I think I know exactly the tattoo. Get dressed." Colton helped her off his lap.

Vida tried not to look worried when she remembered they hadn't worn a condom. "I always wore a condom with the other women, Vida. I swear I wouldn't put your health at risk," he said when Vida couldn't hide her worry.

"I believe you. Luckily, I'm on the pill because I cramp

so bad when I'm on my period." Colton didn't look happy at her news. "I thought you would be relieved there wouldn't be a chance of me getting pregnant." Colton shrugged, pulling on his jeans.

"I wouldn't have been upset. I like kids."

"I do, too." Vida carried her clothes into the bathroom across the hall from Colton's room. Cleaning herself, she then dressed before coming back into his room. She found him sitting on his stool, ready to start.

Vida sat down in the chair. "Give me your hand," Colton demanded, holding out his own.

Vida placed her hand in his. He turned it over, wiping down the back of her wrist before he began outlining the tattoo. This time, Vida had a clear view of how he worked.

"Don't you get tired of giving tattoos?" Vida asked curiously.

"No, it relaxes me. I enjoy doing it. Trying to come up with designs for people that I've just met is challenging."

"What's the worst tattoo you've ever given?"

Colton worked steadily. "Max. He kept bugging me to give him a big tattoo on his back. Wanted it to cover his whole back. I kept putting him off, but one night he finally wore me down and I tatted him."

"What did you do?"

"Well, we both were drunk. I thought I had done quite a bit of work, but we both must have passed out. We woke up the next day and he came to my room to show me what I had tatted on him."

"What was it?"

"A tramp stamp."

"You didn't." Vida giggled.

"I did." The man went fucking crazy on me. I barely managed to escape with my life. He wouldn't even let me touch him to do the cover up. He got another artist to do it for him."

"He seemed so easy going. I can't imagine him that angry."

"Baby, they call him Max. That's his nickname," Colton explained.

"It isn't much of one. The nickname Max is kind of boring."

"Think about it. Max, as in, "Mad Max"."

"Oh."

"Yeah. He gave me a black eye that lasted a good month, not to mention he destroyed my room."

"Wow."

"Don't piss him off," Colton warned.

"I won't."

Colton worked steadily for an hour before he finished, wiping down her wrist with a clean cloth. He scooted his stool back to watch her reaction.

"What do you think?"

Vida looked down at the back of her wrist. Tears clogged her throat. Blue forget-me-nots. There were vines twined down, buried in the flowers. You could see three names; Sawyer, Callie and Colton.

He had given her his name twice now. Vida knew he was telling her how much she meant to him.

"I couldn't think of one single thing more perfect than this night, Colton. Every time I look at this, I'll remember everyone I love."

Callie's name and the flowers together had a trace of a memory stirring.

"What's wrong?" Colton took her wrist, wrapping it carefully.

"I don't know." Vida frowned. "Last night, Briggs told me Sawyer had been taken because of our connection to King. Colton, other than my mother working for him, there is no connection. I don't understand."

She could tell it wasn't the first time he had heard the same comment. "When I starting asking around, I found out the same thing, Vida. King had a protection order out on both you and Sawyer. After his sister, only someone determined to provoke King would have touched either of you."

"I don't understand." Vida watched Colton clean his room.

"There has to be something we're missing. Let's go. It's late, and you need some food and sleep."

She nodded, automatically following him as they left.

On the ride home, Vida did nothing other than try to think about King, searching her mind and coming up blank.

Colton fixed their dinner while Vida showered.

She worried that something she had forgotten might hurt Sawyer's safety. Vida washed her hair, wanting desperately for this whole mess to be over, but a deep, dark fear was growing inside of her, warning her it was just beginning.

Chapter Eighteen

Vida woke the next morning to find Colton sound asleep. They had gone to bed after dinner. Vida had tried to make up the couch, however Colton had convinced her with several smoldering kisses that sharing his bed was the more pleasurable option.

Her sore body told her that she needed a hot shower. Quietly, not wanting to wake Colton, she went into the shower where the hot water soothed her aching muscles. Running the soapy sponge over her body, Vida jumped when the shower door opened unexpectedly.

"Colton, get out." Vida tried to turn away.

Colton ignored her protests, coming into the shower to stand behind her.

"Son-of-a-bitch. That water is hot," Colton grumbled.

"Then get out," Vida ordered.

"Baby, I've seen and touched everything you have last night. Why so shy about taking a shower with me?"

"A shower is private."

"There's nothing private anymore. I am going to learn everything about you and you're going to learn everything about me."

"I don't know if I want you to learn all my secrets." Vida turned so the water could wash away the soap.

"Don't get your tat wet," Colton warned. His hand on her ass enforced his message.

Vida jumped, throwing him a dirty look. He grinned back, reaching out to take away the soapy sponge and running it over her body.

"I've already washed," she protested.

"I think you missed a spot." Colton's hand went between her legs where the soft sponge brushed against her tender pussy. Vida was unable to prevent herself from spreading her legs wider when he rubbed harder against her clit. Reaching out, she braced a hand against his shoulder as she felt herself getting more excited from the friction he created. Looking downward, she saw his cock hard and slick.

"Colton…"

He shook his head. "You're too sore." Denying her made her want him more.

"Please, Colton. I need you." She took his cock in her hand, stroking him slowly at first then building her speed until he had to brace a hand on the shower wall. Her hand fell away.

"Come here." Colton's restraint broke,

Pushing her up against the shower wall, he raised one of her legs to his hips. His cock pierced her with one hard thrust. The exquisite pain had Vida biting down on his shoulder.

"Motherfucker," Colton hissed, shoving more of himself deep within her.

Vida went wild, fighting him for control, driving her hips against him as he thrust inside of her, searching for and finding the motion that brought her the most pleasure. She moaned as she finally managed to convince Colton to give her what she needed. He pounded inside her with a series of hard thrusts while her arms circled his shoulders and her head fell back against the shower wall.

"Harder, Colton. Fuck me harder." Colton thrust higher, bringing her over the edge. Her rippling pussy gripped his cock, catching him unprepared for the climax he couldn't hold back, forcing a hard groan from his own throat.

Afterwards, he washed her again and then carefully helped her trembling body out of the shower. Vida couldn't quit shaking. Colton dried her off then lifted her into his arms, carrying her back to the bed. Lying down next to her, he pulled her into his arms.

"I understand now," Vida whispered out loud.

"What?" Colton turned his head to look at her.

"My mother. I've been judging her like a kid." Vida had been judgmental where her mother had been concerned, always looking at it from her own point-of-view and not her mothers. "She was searching for this, wasn't she?"

"Yes, your mom was the most giving woman I had ever met until you. In that respect, you take after her. She was a wonderful person. She wanted a man that she could love in her life. She just wasn't lucky enough to find him."

Vida stared up at the ceiling. Her life had been planned out, and she had been so sure of what she wanted. Since she had met Colton, though, she felt as if everything was changing. Pulling away, she got out of bed and got dressed. Ignoring Colton's frown, she brushed her hair before braiding it back.

"What are you doing?"

"I need to wash some clothes, and I'm hungry. We need groceries." Vida named several things they needed to get done on their day off.

"Okay. Food first then we will get busy with everything else." Vida watched as he dressed, regretting that she had put an end to their fuckfest, yet she needed some time to figure out what she was doing.

They decided to have breakfast out, sharing a huge stack of pancakes and laughing at who had the bigger appetite. Afterwards, they went grocery shopping. Vida picked out several items that would be easy to prepare after working in the shop all day while Colton picked out items that could be microwaved and were tasteless. Those, Vida put back.

"Hey, I wanted those burritos," Colton complained.

"No, you didn't." Vida pushed the grocery cart on, leaving him behind.

"I did."

"Stuff like that won't fill you up, it'll make you fat." Vida pushed the cart to the fresh fruit. Picking out a variety of apples and oranges, she put those in the cart.

Colton put several more items in the cart, most were rejected and put back by Vida.

"I'm getting my cereal," Colton protested when she placed it back on the shelf.

"We don't need it. We have oatmeal and the frozen pancakes that you wanted."

"Vida, I'm not giving my cereal up."

"Colton, you'll..."

"And I won't get fat because I plan to work off the calories fucking you."

Vida closed her mouth and put the cereal back in the buggy.

They had walked to the nearby grocery store. Carrying the groceries back to the apartment, Vida smiled.

"What's so funny?" Colton asked.

"I swore I wouldn't end up like my mother, yet here I am, packing groceries back to an apartment three blocks away from where I grew up."

"Fate's a bitch."

"Yes, she is." Coming to an intersection, they stopped, waiting for the light to turn red so they could cross. The traffic halted as the light turned red. Out of the corner of her eye she saw a little boy on his bike on the sidewalk riding towards the road. His was trying to stop, however he was going too fast. He was going to run out in front of the traffic that had begun moving from the other direction now that their light was green.

Vida instinctively dropped her grocery bags and started running. Screaming when she realized she wasn't going to reach the child in time. Colton ran past her, barely managing to reach the child before a car slammed on its brakes.

The child's mother ran out of one the shops, crying frantically at the same time that she thanked Colton. He lifted the bike back on the sidewalk and handed the child to his mother, assuring her he was fine.

"Thank God," Vida said when Colton came back to her side.

"Let's get the groceries," Colton said grimly.

Luckily, they hadn't purchased anything that could have been broken.

Shakily, Vida walked the rest of the way home where Colton took the bags from her and then Vida sat down at the kitchen table while Colton grabbed her a bottled water from the fridge.

"You saved that child's life," she said shakily.

Colton shook his head. "I didn't even see what was happening until you took off running. You saved him, I didn't. That mother owes his life to you." Vida, about to raise the bottled water to her lips, stopped. A memory that she had forgotten came to life, playing back in her mind.

"Vida?" Colton quit putting up the groceries, watching her as realization dawned on her face.

"I remember, Colton. I remember something about King." Colton sat down next to her at the table.

"What did you remember?"

"When we were little, Sawyer, Callie and I were outside playing one day on the playground." It hadn't been a normal playground; it had a couple of slides and a merry-go-round that didn't work. They would usually sit on it instead of the dirt to play with their dolls. That was, Sawyer and her would play with their dolls, Callie didn't have any. The girls would share with her, but she never had one of her own.

"One day, Callie showed up with a brand new doll. She was so proud of it. Both Sawyer and I wanted to play with it. She was so sweet, Colton. That was the first toy I had ever seen her with, yet she shared it with us.

"We were having such a good time. I can't believe I forgot this, Colton. I still see her playing with that doll."

"You probably blocked it out because your memories of her are so painful." Colton took her hand.

Vida held it tightly, continuing her story, "There was a gang of boys who were bugging us, especially Sawyer. She had Callie's doll and one of the boys jerked it from her hand and threw it into the street. Callie took off running into the street. Sawyer and I ran after her, both of us reached her just before a car drove over the doll, crushing it. If we hadn't reached her in time, she would have been killed. That car was going so fast…" Vida's voice broke off.

"What does this have to do with King?"

"He came running from our apartment building like the mother did today with the same look on his face. He was terrified. He yelled at all three of us, saying we could have been killed."

"Did he pay attention to any one of you in particular?"

"No, he just took us back to the playground and gave those boys hell. Scared them all into running home."

"Is that all you remember?" Colton asked.

"I think so. I think he said something to Sawyer, but I don't remember. I couldn't hear him very well because Callie was crying so hard about losing her doll and I was holding her, but Sawyer heard because I saw her say something back. He left after that. But Colton, after that day, no one bugged us again. When those boys saw us again, they would always go inside."

"Vida, what do you know about your father?"

"Not much, my mom got pregnant when she was fourteen, had me when she was fifteen. My dad was seventeen. They lived together until I was born then he went back to his family. She said he was killed in a car accident, driving an expensive car his parents had given him for leaving us."

"Goldie told me the same thing. What do you know about Sawyer's father?"

"Sawyer's mother and father were married, he was killed when Sawyer was a baby. That's why her mother was so overprotective. She hardly ever let Sawyer out of her sight. Do you think King could be her father and that her mother lied? That could be another reason for her over-protectiveness."

"I don't know. Did Callie ever talk about her father?"

At that, Vida rolled her eyes. "She didn't even know what a daddy was until we explained it to her when she was four-years-old. But I can't imagine King touching Callie's mom, could you?"

Colton shook his head. "No, even I hated the bitch, what little I knew of her."

"He couldn't be Callie's father. He wouldn't have watched how Callie was treated and not step up, would he?"

"I don't know. His sister's death hit him hard," Colton answered, running his hands through his hair. "If what we're thinking is true, Digger may have found out that one of the three of you is King's daughter."

"I've seen pictures of my dad, Colton. I really don't think King's my father. I kind of look like my father, from the pictures I've seen."

"Then it has to be either Sawyer or Callie. Callie is in the ground where no one can touch her anymore. If it's Sawyer and Digger finds out, or already figured it out, you won't be getting her back."

Vida tried not to cry, but was unsuccessful. Her fear for Sawyer overcoming her desire to stay strong. Colton pulled her onto his lap. "I'll call King. We'll have to get him to tell us the truth. It won't be easy, Vida."

Vida nodded her head, trying to get her emotions under control. "You finish putting up the groceries while I call King."

Colton was still on the phone when she finished putting away the remaining groceries so she started doing the laundry. She gathered some of Colton's and her own clothes and started a load in the washer.

She returned to the living room to find Colton still talking into the phone. Vida could tell from his face it wasn't good news. Disconnecting the call, Colton picked up his bike keys.

"What's wrong?"

"King isn't answering his phone. I called the club; he's not in his room and no one as seen him since last night. Ice called and said we need to get over to the clubhouse, now."

"Sawyer?" Vida asked, frightened.

"He didn't give me any info, just told us to hurry."

Vida rushed to the door with Colton behind her. Colton didn't drive recklessly, but he didn't stick to the speed limit, either. She prayed the whole way there that they didn't get pulled over. A parole violation was the last thing they needed right now.

Colton pulled in front of a large building on the outskirts of town with a large number of motorcycles out front and parked his bike at the back of the building. Taking Vida's hand, they walked to the backdoor. Knocking, it took only a minute before a large woman with grayish, black hair answered the door. Her frown turned into a smile as she opened the door wider and jerked Colton forward into a hug.

Vida laughed when the woman tossed him aside and punched him on his arm.

"You pussy, just now coming to see us, and you been out a few weeks."

"Gert, you know it's better I stay away…"

"Afraid they'll send you back to prison? In my day, I

would have pulled my time. I wouldn't have had to deal with no parole," the woman bragged.

"Did they have cars and airplanes back then or were people still riding horses?" Colton joked.

"I'll shove a horse up your ass," Gert mock threatened.

Vida couldn't keep from laughing, turning the woman's attention towards her.

"Who's the bitch?"

Vida stiffened, ready to snap a remark back at the woman.

This time it was Colton laughing. Putting an arm around Vida's shoulder, he pulled her close to his side.

"This is Vida."

"She's pretty. What does she want with your ass?"

Colton smiled, answering her question without words. Vida wanted to strangle him.

"Go on in. Ice is waiting for you. Your bitch can wait out here with the others and me.

"But I want…" Vida interrupted.

"Doesn't matter what you want. No women are allowed in church. Go on, Colton, I got this."

"I won't be long," he said before disappearing behind a door to the side of them.

"Come on, I'll show you around." Gert's no nonsense attitude left Vida without a choice.

Gert led her into a large room with several chairs, two pool tables and a large bar with several bar stools. A large group of women were sitting in the oversized chairs, talking. They were all of various ages; several seemed to be her own age or younger, but there were many who were older.

They stopped talking when Gert entered the room with her.

"This is Colton's old lady, so you bitches better behave," she threatened the women. "You want a beer?" she asked Vida.

"Thanks." Right now Vida needed all the alcohol she

could get with the women all staring at her.

Gert went behind the bar before coming back with a cold beer, handing it to her. "Thank you."

"Well, isn't she polite," a blond said snidely.

"Better watch your mouth," a pretty brunette said, getting up and coming forward.

"Why do we have to kiss her ass? Colton's not a member anymore. Dumb fuck got caught..." A loud smack across her face had her falling backward into the chair she was sitting on. Gert was standing over her.

"I told you to be nice, bitch." The blond shut up, holding her cheek.

"That's Rita, and I'm Crush." Vida smiled at the pretty brunette. "Have a seat, and I'll introduce everyone else. Vida took an empty seat next to a young looking girl, wondering if she was even eighteen.

"Hi, I'm Rave."

As the other women introduced themselves, Vida wasn't sure she would remember their names, she was so nervous.

"How did you meet Colton?" Rave asked. Vida told them about her meeting Colton at the strip club and even the women that had given her a cool reception seemed to defrost.

Rita came to sit next to her. "I didn't realize you were a sister. From the way you were dressed, I thought you were a stuck up cow. I stripped, too, before I met Lizard. He didn't like a bunch of strangers staring at my tits."

"He doesn't mind if every man in the club sees them," Gert taunted.

"That's different." Rita shrugged her shoulders.

"Yeah, he knows you're a slut," Gert interrupted again.

"Old woman, I'll pull that grey hair out of your head for free if you don't shut the fuck up."

Gert leaned back in her chair laughing. "Come and get me."

Rita ignored her, turning back to Vida. They were still

talking when the men came into the room. Colton came under attack from several of the women, each trying to get his attention. Several even kissed him on the mouth, taking turns. Vida's blood was beginning to boil.

"Calm down, they're just saying hi," Gert said by her side.

"They don't have to use their tongue to do it," Vida replied sharply.

Colton, seeing her, broke free from the women and came to her side. He curled his arm around her waist and pulled her close as Ice and Max managed to edge through the crowd.

"Vida, you remember Ice and Max?" Another man came to stand by Ice. "That's Buzzard. He's Ice's vice-president.

Vida acknowledged each man, her eyes on the one behind the group with the scar.

Colton's arm tightened on her when he saw who she was staring at.

"That's Jackal. He's Ice's sergeant-at-arms."

"Why did Ice need to see you?" Vida dragged her attention from the club members, concerned for Sawyer's safety.

"Ice wanted to tell me what went down last night. Seems the FBI hit the recording studio, the basement had about ten women held there, and they were in bad shape. A couple of Digger's men were arrested. Digger was there, but he managed to escape."

"No." Vida couldn't believe the slimy bastard managed to get away.

"Yes, stupid fucks let him slip through their fucking fingers. Now he's blaming King for ratting him out and he's determined to get back at him then kill him, in that order," Ice confirmed her worst fear.

"How do you know?"

No one answered.

Vida remembered what Seth had told her about Digger

having some friends left in the Predators. Vida was willing to bet that one or two were merely pretending to maintain an eye on what Digger was up to. Then another thought occurred to her.

"Digger will go after Sawyer," Vida whispered. If there was a connection to King, he would kill Sawyer. "We have to find her."

"We already have the word out. It's going to take time." From his voice, Ice didn't hold out much hope.

Vida turned toward Colton, burying her face in his chest, not wanting anyone to see her crying.

"We'll find her, baby." Colton tried to give her hope, but Vida knew from losing Callie that sometime help came too late.

They stayed until it grew dark. Colton stood at the bar with his friends, laughing and joking around. He had lost a lot when he had gone to prison for Tessa. He had a life, friends and a business he had sacrificed so the woman he had married and who had carried his child wouldn't suffer.

"He's a nice guy," Gert said next to her.

"Yes, I'm finding that out," agreed Vida.

"One woman has already fucked him over. I understand your friend is in trouble, but I don't want Colton to get himself in trouble again trying to protect another woman."

Vida stared at Colton. Gert was right, he had no stake in this. He was only involved because of her. "I won't let him get hurt," Vida promised.

"If you do, I'm going to kick your ass," Gert promised with a hard glare.

"Okay." Vida was going to make sure that Colton wasn't hurt, whatever it took, although it had very little to do with Gert's promise.

"What are you both looking so serious about?" Colton asked, handing Vida another beer.

"I'm telling her she needs to get some sexier clothes if she's going to be your bitch," Gert lied.

"I like her just the way she is. Leave her alone, Gert."

"I will. If she takes my advice," she said with a meaningful look.

"You ready?"

"Yes," Vida answered.

Colton went to tell Ice they were leaving while Vida said goodbye to Rita, Crush and the other women. As they left, she caught Ice and Jackal's eyes on her. She had a feeling that they had the same idea as Gert, that she was leading Colton down the same path Tessa had. Vida was going to prove them wrong.

Chapter Nineteen

When they returned to the apartment, Vida dried the clothes she had washed earlier and started another load. Colton didn't volunteer to fold the clothes when she dried the second load, but he did rub lotion onto her tattoo. Vida figured it was an even trade.

"Do you think Tessa will show up for work tomorrow?" Vida asked, watching for his reaction.

"Not if she's smart," he said grimly.

"It doesn't matter, Colton. If she wants to come back, let her. I feel sorry for her."

Colton looked at her as if she was crazy.

"I do. I don't know that I would act much better if I saw you with another woman," she confessed.

"You wouldn't lie. You would get mad and probably throw something, but you wouldn't lie. Roni would have told her the truth, that I never touched Goldie. Tessa always lies, either to cause trouble or get out of trouble. She never tells the truth."

Vida couldn't understand why the woman had destroyed her marriage for drugs. Instead of owning up to it to try to save her marriage, she had lied. Even more, selling herself to keep the lie going.

Tired, Vida showered and dressed in her pajamas. She came out to find Colton waiting for her on the bed with a wicked grin.

"Oh no, you don't. I'm tired and sore," Vida said adamantly.

Colton held out his arms for her and Vida sank down into them. "I like this."

"I do, too," Colton replied. "Of course, I like the other, too."

Vida's eyes closed. "Did you try to call King again?"

"Yes, he's still not answering and no one has seen him at the club."

"Could Digger have him?" Vida was worried. Even though King was ruthless, he had tried to help when no one else would.

"I don't know. We'll just have to wait for now," Colton replied.

Wait. That was all she had been doing the last few weeks. She was getting sick of it.

Vida's mind went back over that day that Callie was almost hit by the car, trying to figure out what she'd missed. It was impossible; it had been too long ago for her to remember the details of that day perfectly enough. The only way to find out was to find Sawyer. She was the only possibility of figuring out how King was involved in this mess. They had to find Sawyer, she was the answer.

* * *

Vida volunteered to get coffee across the street while Colton opened the shop.

"Don't be long."

"I won't." Vida crossed the street.

The coffee shop was busy with the line out the door. She was about to turn away, not wanting to worry Colton, when she heard the sound of a car slamming on their brakes. The car had swerved in front of the coffee shop parking haphazardly.

Wondering what the hurry was for a cup of coffee, Vida recognized the woman getting out of the car and waving at her.

"Vida, come here!" Ashley yelled when Vida didn't move toward her.

"What are you doing? That car almost hit you," Vida said, noticing the woman wasn't wearing make-up and looked scared to death.

"Get in. I need to talk to you," Ashley said, getting back inside her car. Vida hesitated, but got inside the car. The woman looked too frightened for Vida to ignore.

"What's wrong?" Vida asked as soon as she was in the car.

"King's disappeared."

"I know. I've been trying to get in touch with him."

"He disappeared after that stunt we pulled with Briggs."

"That same night?"

"He was furious when I came downstairs and told him what Briggs told me. He took off, and no one's seen him since. I heard about Briggs getting arrested and Digger getting away. I may not be the smartest cookie in the pack, but I'm smart enough to get my ass out of town, and you should, too. I don't plan on ending up like those poor women in that basement. I can't be a sex slave. I don't even like sex with men. I like women more than men." The woman was giving more information than Vida wanted or needed.

"Slow down, Ashley. Tell me what Briggs told you."

"After you left, he drank some more. I couldn't understand half of what he was talking about, but then he started talking about a chick named Sawyer. Sherri told me the only reason you were stripping was to help your friend Sawyer. I didn't figure there were two women named Sawyer, so I knew he was talking about your friend."

"What did he say?" Vida tried to keep her on track.

"He just said a name over and over. Said King would

never find her."

"What was the name?"

Ashley reached into her pocket and held out a piece of paper. "I don't know what it means and I don't want to. I'm moving back in with my parents. If you want my advice, Vida, it's to get out of town at least until King shows back up at the club. If he does."

Ashley put the car in gear. Vida took the hint, getting out of the car, and watched as Ashley pulled out, cutting off another furious driver.

Vida opened the piece of paper, reading the name on it. She drew a blank, not knowing what it meant. *Mouth2Mouth*. However she did know where she could find the answer.

Vida rushed into the tattoo shop, ignoring Colton, Reverend and Carlito who all stared at her empty hands.

"Where's the coffee? Colton said you were getting it," Carlito asked.

"I forgot it," Vida said, powering up her computer.

"What's happened?" Colton asked, frowning.

"Ashley was outside. She told me Briggs told her something, but she didn't know what it meant. I'm going to look it up on the internet." She handed him the piece of paper.

Colton opened the paper with both Carlito and Reverend looking over his shoulder.

"What does it mean?" Carlito asked, just when the computer flashed the answer.

"It's a band," Vida answered. Briggs had bragged that Digger provided women to movie and rock stars.

"Why would they be crazy enough to become involved with Briggs?" Colton asked.

"Maybe they don't know. Briggs said that by the time Digger lets them loose, they don't even try to get away anymore," Vida repeated Briggs's words.

"Motherfucker, I want to meet this bastard," Reverend swore.

"Do you think that this band has Sawyer? Digger said whoever had her didn't want to give her back. Musicians have security; that might be why Digger couldn't get her back."

"That makes sense. I think you're right. If Ashley told King, this might be where he's at, trying to find Sawyer." Colton speculated.

"She said he left right after she told him." Vida turned off her computer, packing it back in the bag. Standing up, she saw the men all staring at her.

"Where do you think you're going?" Colton questioned her.

"They have a concert the day after tomorrow. I plan to be there."

"Okay. Reverend, take Vida back to the apartment. Vida, pack us enough clothes to last a week. Carlito, you stay here. I'm going to go see my parole officer, that will give me a week until I have to report again. You'll have to run the shop while I'm gone. I'll cancel all my appointments until I get back."

"You're not going with me." Vida was determined to put a stop to his plans.

"Yes, I am. There's no way you're going by yourself. Not only is King probably headed there, but also Digger. That concert is one big cluster fuck waiting to happen," Colton predicted.

"You're not going. I won't take a chance on you breaking you're parole. I won't be the reason you're sent back to prison," Vida argued back.

"You don't have a choice. I'm going. In fact, I'd like it better if you stayed here. Ice can watch over you until I get back."

"Stop it, Colton." Vida sank back down in the chair. "Neither of us will go, I'll call Seth."

"After everything you've gone through, you're going to give up? You stripped on stage to keep her safe, why would you give up now?"

"I'm not giving up. I just won't jeopardize you going back to jail. I love Sawyer, but I love you, too." A sound in the doorway had everyone turning. Tessa stood, listening to them with the open door in her hand.

"I need to get my machine, and a few other things. Is that all right?" Tessa asked. Vida felt her sympathy stir. Tessa looked like she hadn't slept since the argument with Colton.

"Go ahead, Tessa," Colton said, turning his back on her. Tessa didn't try to talk to the other two men as she went on back to her room. Vida felt Colton's gaze on her the whole time. The door opened again and clients began coming in.

"Go to work, Colton. I'll call Seth as soon as I get everyone checked in and let him know what's going on. The room was bugged that night; they probably are already moving to get Sawyer back, maybe that's why Seth hasn't called me."

"All right, but come to me as soon as you talk to him."

"I will," Vida agreed.

The men got to work with their appointments. Tessa came into the lobby, pausing beside the counter. Vida looked back at her, waiting for the nastiness to spill out of her.

"I'm sorry for the other day," Tessa said.

Shocked was an understatement to what Vida felt when she heard Tessa's words.

"I understand, Tessa. I don't think I would take it well if I lost Colton, either."

"I lost Colton because I couldn't admit I had a problem. I went to rehab, went through all the steps, yet I never apologized to Colton and he was the one I hurt the most."

"It's not too late, Tessa."

"Yes, it is." Vida watched as Tessa walked out the front door, not taking the opportunity to go back and apologize to Colton. Vida had hoped that Tessa would try to make amends, but she had been wrong.

Vida kept trying to get Seth on the phone, using the number he'd given her. His message box was full. She was beginning to get angry with him. The least he could do was keep her informed after what she had done.

Determined to get in touch with him, she called the FBI's main office for the State of Texas. It took several phone calls and being redirected several times before she was connected to a nearby office. in which Seth had been assigned.

"Hello?" Vida had asked for Seth and had met silence on the other end. "Hello? Are you still there?"

"Yes, Ms.--. I'm afraid I have some bad news about your friend. Seth Redman was killed on duty. I'm afraid that's all the information that can be released at this time."

Vida disconnected the call, sitting stunned.

"Are you all right?" Carlito asked, picking up the appointment book.

"Yes." Vida cleared her throat. "I need some coffee and some food. I'm going to go across the street. I'll be back in a little while."

"Cool, I don't have another customer for an hour. Take your time."

"Thanks." Vida packed up her computer, placing it into her backpack.

Carlito waved to her as she left, already texting his girlfriend, which was his favorite pastime when he wasn't working.

Vida crossed the street in front of the tattoo shop, went in front of the coffee shop and then kept walking. Around the corner, she called a taxi. Vida waited anxiously for five minutes for it to arrive. Finally, the cab pulled up and Vida climbed in, giving Colton's address.

It took another agonizing ten minutes for the cab to get to Colton's apartment. Carlito hadn't even noticed when she had picked up Colton's keys. He was going to be furious when he realized she had the bike and apartment keys. It wouldn't take a genius to figure out where she was headed, but she planned to call him as soon as possible and beg him not to follow.

Thankfully, all her clothes were clean. She shoved everything into the small case she had. Picking up her backpack, she was in the bedroom when she heard the front door open. Freezing in place by the bed, she watched the bedroom door.

Colton entered the bedroom, furious. Vida knew she was busted trying to leave town without him and he was mad as hell at her.

"What the hell were you thinking?" he yelled at her.

He walked towards her, stopping by the bed when he saw her clothes packed in the case. Angrily, he picked the suitcase up and threw it across the room. The backpack was next, and she could tell from his face it was going to meet the same fate as her suitcase.

"Don't you dare throw that backpack. It has my computer that I had to save for three semester's to buy used."

Colton gently tossed the backpack onto the floor by the bed.

Vida couldn't help the giggle that escaped her. Colton might have saved her computer, but he was still furious with her. Picking her up, he tossed her onto the mattress, coming down on top of her before she could scramble off.

"I can't let you violate your parole, Colton. Let me handle it, please. It's my problem, not yours. You got dragged into this whole mess because of King."

"Baby, calm down. We're going back to my original plan. After I see my parole officer, he won't expect me for another week. We'll be back by then."

"What if you get pulled over by the police or there's trouble and they run your license? Anything could go wrong. I won't take that chance."

"You don't have a choice." Colton ignored her arguing.

"You'll hate me if you get caught," Vida protested.

"I couldn't hate you, Vida. You're fierce in your loyalty to Sawyer, and you've worked hard for your degree to get what you want out of life. I understand that both are important to you. I'm not going to let you leave to find Sawyer on your own. When we find Sawyer then we'll decide what's next, but whatever it is, it doesn't mean I'm going to let you leave without me."

"I don't want to leave you, either. I even applied for jobs in Queen City and I've wanted to leave all my life. But I want to stay because of you."

"I can start a tattoo shop anywhere, Vida. I don't even have to tattoo. I have plenty of money saved up; I've lived real tight the last few years," he said with a twisted smile. "We can go anywhere you want, for as long as you want. The only thing I need is you, nothing else matters."

"I don't mind Queen City so much anymore, and all your friends are here. Sawyer is my only friend and the fun of leaving was to have that experience with her." Vida couldn't keep the sadness out of her voice.

"Were going to get her back, I promise." Vida pulled him to her, kissing him for promising something he had no control over.

"Did you mean what you said in the shop this morning?" he asked, staring into her eyes.

"No," Vida lied, lowering her eyes so he couldn't see the answer she wasn't able to hide.

"Baby…"

"Yes, I meant it." Vida buried her face in his shoulder, embarrassed.

"I love you, too. I did from the moment I saw you on stage. I thought I had died and gone to Heaven."

Vida hit at his shoulder. Well aware that the first time he had seen her, she was stripping.

"The first time you saw me I was naked."

"Yes, you were. I saw…" Colton kissed her as his hands went under her t-shirt, pushing it up over her breasts. Unsnapping her bra, he sucked a nipple into his

200

mouth, pressing it hard between his lips until Vida's hand went to his long hair and she began twisting underneath him. Switching to the other breast he unexpectedly used his piercing to rub the tip. It hardened into a perfect pink bud. "…these pretty pink nipples."

He got up from the bed and then, reaching down, he unsnapped her jeans, tugging them and her panties off in one movement. Cupping her behind the knees, he pulled her towards the end of the bed. "This pretty, wet pussy… was all I could think about for days after I saw your show."

"I could tell," Vida said wryly, remembering how many women had shared his bed when he first got out of prison.

"Their nipples weren't as pink as yours." Leaning over her, he took a nipple between his fingertips, pinching and twisting gently until Vida's hips squirmed on the bed. Letting it go, he reached for the other nipple, playing with it until Vida started rubbing herself against the front of him. His cock lengthened behind his unbuttoned jeans.

Releasing her nipple, he straightened once again.

"Their pussies weren't as tight as yours." Colton thrust a finger into her already wet pussy. Vida's hips thrust back needing to feel him thick and full inside of her. He was only giving her touches to drive her passion higher.

"Colton, I need you," Vida whimpered.

"They damn sure didn't taste like you." Vida whimpered again, knowing what was next. Colton raised her up to his mouth. The only part of her left on the bed was the back of her head.

Colton wrapped her calves around his shoulder and went down on her already wet clit, his tongue laving, wringing moans from her as he drove her mindlessly into a climax which he let her ride out on his tongue. She hadn't stopped shaking when he lowered her hips back to the mattress. Spreading her thighs wider, he notched his cock at her entrance.

"Fuck me. Please, just fuck me," Vida begged him unashamedly.

Colton slid his cock in her wet heat before thrusting fully inside. Vida arched as he slid deeper, moving in an out in a slow rhythm that had her thrusting back, trying to get him to go faster.

"Harder. I need it harder," Vida begged.

Colton used his palm to pull back her mound until her clit rested on his cock.

"Baby, I'm always going to give you what you ask for." He thrust high and hard within her, holding her shoulders to the bed. Each thrust rubbed her clit, sending shards of pleasure inside of her that were so intense that she was unable to hold back the climax storming her body. Her wildly bucking hips had him lowering his body over hers as his thrusts became harder, capturing and sharing the same orgasm which became as primal as it was loving. He gave her the essence of himself with a final thrust, committing his body and soul as she gave hers in return.

"That was beautiful," Vida whispered, unable to stop clinging to him.

"That was how I felt when I first saw you..." Colton said, not wanting her to let him go.

Chapter Twenty

Vida stood nervously by Colton as he knocked on his parole officer's door. Colton opened the door when the voice told him to come inside. She had wanted to wait outside, but Colton had refused to let her leave his side. Giving in, she now found herself under the scrutiny of a large man behind a desk. If his hair hadn't been black and long, worn in a ponytail, he would have been a ringer for Santa. However, the man sitting behind the desk had anything other than a jolly look on his ruddy face.

"Dax, I wanted to check in today, I have several appointments scheduled for tomorrow. I had to fire one of my artists so I'm short staffed," Colton explained to the man, who from the looks he was giving Colton, could care less about his explanations.

Dax leaned back in his chair. "Is that right?"

"Yes." Colton gave the probation officer a sharp look. Vida was beginning to feel that he also was sensing that something wasn't right.

"Aren't you going to introduce us, Colton?"

"Dax Carter, this is Vida Bell. She's my fiancée." Vida looked at him in surprise. She must have been asleep when he'd proposed because she damn sure didn't remember it.

"You don't waste much time, do you, Colton? The ink's barely dry on your divorce papers and you already have a new fiancée."

"Maybe not, but they are signed and it's legal," Colton countered.

"Have a seat, Colton. You too, Ms. Bell," Dax said, pulling open a folder on his desk.

"I'm glad you stopped by. I had to change your schedule, and now that you're here, it saves me the trouble of emailing it to you." Dax leaned forward, handing Colton a piece of paper that he picked up off his desk. Colton took it from him.

Vida began to get worried when Colton took several minutes, reading over it. She had promised she wouldn't leave without him to find Sawyer. If his probation schedule didn't give them enough time to get to Indiana and back, then he wouldn't be able to go. She wouldn't break her promise to him, which meant she could lose Sawyer forever.

"I don't understand." Colton's hoarse voice drew Vida's mind away from her worried thoughts.

"Let me explain it for you. This morning, your ex-wife went to the police with her lawyer and confessed to the crime you committed. She is now under arrest, since she is yet to be convicted, all charges against you cannot be dropped. Your lawyer, who was notified, is currently taking care of all the necessary paperwork. I should wait until this gets the judge's approval, but I see no need for further visits pending the judge's approval. In plain words, you're a free man."

"Tessa confessed?" Colton asked.

"Yes, she even included in the statement that you were under emotional duress because she was carrying your child," Dax explained to a shaken Colton.

"I can't believe after all this time, she confessed," Colton said unbelievably.

"It's her way of telling you she's sorry," Vida whispered, her throat tight.

"It's a little late if you ask me. She could have saved him three years in prison," Dax said, clearly unimpressed with Tessa's gesture.

"It's not too late." Vida stood up, hugging Colton when he rose from his chair. Tessa had made it possible for them to leave town without having to worry about Colton getting in trouble for a parole violation.

Colton reached across the desk and shook his parole officer's hand. They turned towards the door.

"Colton, if by some chance you decide to leave town and run into any difficulty, give them my card." Colton and Vida both stopped, turning back to Dax. "I've been a parole officer a long time, no one shows up early for an appointment."

"Thanks, Dax." Vida waited for Colton to close the door behind them before throwing herself in his arms again.

"Let's drop the keys off to Reverend then we can hit the road," Colton said as they got on his bike.

The parole office was a twenty minute ride away from the tattoo shop.

They pulled in the lot just as the last client left.

Reverend was waiting for them inside.

"I sent Carlito home. The boy's going to need his rest. I told him he's working full-time until you get back."

"He can handle it; he's a good artist, almost as good as you at his age," Colton complimented his friend.

Colton handed Reverend the shop keys. "Thanks, Reverend. Take care of it for me until I get back."

"You know I will, brother. Be safe."

"Always." Vida laughed at the man hug they gave each other before hugging Reverend herself.

"You two better be going, not much daylight left," Reverend warned.

Vida turned to go outside, coming to an abrupt stop.

"Uh... Colton?"

"Yeah?" Colton turned, grinning at the sight outside.

Vida followed Colton out the door. The Predators took over the whole parking lot. There were well over a hundred bikes, some even had to park on the street in front of the other businesses.

"What's up, Ice?" Colton said, shaking Ice's hand.

"Reverend gave me a call, telling me you're headed out of town to find your old lady's friend. We've been bored sitting on our asses lately, thought we'd tag along for the ride."

Vida looked at the crew of rough men waiting to ride with them. "Digger couldn't get Sawyer away from this musician because he had security. Want to bet we have better luck?" Vida joked with Colton.

"Sounds like Vida wants your help. Thanks, brother."

Ice nodded his head.

The men all moved their bikes back into position as Vida put on her helmet and climbed onto the back of Colton's bike. When he started his motor, backing the bike up in position, Ice moved forward to pull his bike next to Colton's.

"You might want this to keep you warm." Vida saw Ice hand Colton a leather jacket that looked like the one's the other men wore.

Colton took it from him, pulling on the jacket he had taken off over three years ago.

Vida leaned forward to hear his words. "Baby, you ready for this long ride?" Vida knew he was talking about the ride to Indiana, but she was looking further down the road, to the years ahead.

"I'm ready." Whether they got Sawyer back safely or not, Vida knew she was ready to take whatever road life had in store for Colton and her. They had each other now, and however exciting and dangerous it was, their love would survive the test of time.

Epilogue

Vida walked quickly through the strip club. Her trembling fingers tightened on the belt around her waist. Going up the staircase carefully, she didn't want to trip in the high platform shoes she was wearing and break her neck.

The VIP room had just a few customers already being taken care of by the regular servers.

"You're late. Your client's been out here twice to see if you were here yet," Henry said impassively.

"Sorry," Vida mumbled, going for the private door. She slipped inside, closing and locking the door before taking a deep breath and turning to her client.

"I'm going to kill you for this."

"Is that any way to talk to your client?" Colton laughed.

"If any parents from Axel and Roxi's school recognizes me, you're dead," Vida threatened.

"Vida, baby, I hate to tell you this, but you're kinda putting a damper on my fantasy, talking about the kids." Colton leaned back against his plush chair. "It's your own fault, promising me anything for our anniversary."

"I didn't think you would choose this," she said

through gritted teeth.

"Again, you're killing my buzz. Henry even made sure there are clean sheets on the bed."

Vida turned bright red, unable to prevent herself from looking at the huge bed against the wall.

"Come on, where's the woman I met and fell in love with?"

Gracefully, giving in to her husband's fantasy, Vida reached out, pressing the button by the door. The room filled with Colton and her favorite song. "Resuscitate Me."

Loosening her belt, she unbuttoned her raincoat, showing the three piece stripper outfit she had ordered online.

"Damn woman, you look fine for a soccer mom."

"Now you're ruining my fantasy," Vida reproved him.

"Come here and I'll give you more than a fantasy," Colton promised.

Vida started dancing to the music, edging closer to Colton at the same time that she teased him by removing the top cover of her outfit. Showing the tiny red bra and panties underneath, she leaned over him until her breasts lay against his bare chest.

"Actually, I had a different present in mind for our anniversary," Vida said, straddling his lap.

Colton's eyes were on her swaying breasts as she unsnapped the tiny bra, baring her breasts that had grown fuller with the birth of their children.

"I can't imagine a better present than this," he said, leaning forward to take a nipple between his lips, but Vida evaded him by sitting down on his lap.

"Colton." Her shining eyes and mischievous smile brought a lump to his throat. Taking his hand in hers, she placed it against her bare stomach. "Have you heard the saying double trouble...?"

Also by Jamie Begley

The Last Riders Series:

Razer's Ride

Viper's Run

The VIP Room Series:

Teased

The Dark Souls Series:

Soul Of A Man

About The Author

"I was born in a small town in Kentucky. My family began poor, but worked their way to owning a restaurant. My mother was one of the best cooks I have ever known, and she instilled in all her children the value of hard work, and education.

Taking after my mother, I've always love to cook, and became pretty good if I do say so myself. I love to experiment and my unfortunate family has suffered through many. They now have learned to steer clear of those dishes. I absolutely love the holidays and my family put up with my zany decorations.

For now, my days are spent at work and I write during the nights and weekends. I have two children who both graduate next year from college. My daughter does my book covers, and my son just tries not to blush when someone asks him about my books.

Currently I am writing three series of books- The Last Riders that is fairly popular, The Dark Souls series, which is not, and The VIP Room, which we will soon see. My favorite book I have written is Soul Of A Woman, which I am hoping to release during the summer of 2014. It took me two years to write, during which I lost my mother, and brother. It's a book that I truly feel captures the true depths of love a woman can hold for a man. In case you haven't figured it out yet, I am an emotional writer who wants the readers to feel the emotion of the characters they are reading. Because of this, Teased is probably the hardest thing I have written.

All my books are written for one purpose- the enjoyment others find in them, and the expectations of my fans that inspire me to give it my best. In the near future I hope to take a weekend break and visit Vegas that will hopefully be next summer. Right now I am typing away on Knox's story and looking forward to the coming holidays. Did I mention I love the holidays?"

Jamie loves receiving emails from her fans,
JamieBegley@ymail.com

Find Jamie here,
https://www.facebook.com/AuthorJamieBegley

Get the latest scoop at Jamie's official website,
JamieBegley.net

Printed in Poland
by Amazon Fulfillment
Poland Sp. z o.o., Wrocław